Chinaman's Gold

Leo Denver is in trouble. There's a sick Chinaman back at his ranch, lovely Rose Prescott has married his rival Jake Brody and when Leo tries to drown his sorrows he ends up in jail with the sheriff promising to hang him.

So, when Leo's offered a half share of the Chinaman's gold, he fights his way through the desert to California. A man only gets one crack at winning a fortune. But Jake Brody takes the game into a different league when he murders Leo's brother and captures the Chinaman, Charlie Tang.

Leo must rescue Charlie, but how? And can he beat his enemy to the gold?

Chinaman's Gold

Lou Armstrong

A Black Horse Western

ROBERT HALE · LONDON

ISBN-10: 0-7090-7914-1
ISBN-13: 978-0-7090-7914-9

Robert Hale Limited
Clerkenwell House
Clerkenwell Green
London EC1R 0HT

Typeset by
Derek Doyle & Associates, Shaw Heath.
Printed and bound in Great Britain by
Antony Rowe Limited, Wiltshire

CHAPTER ONE

Live and let live was Leo Denver's motto, so he paid no mind to the group of cowpokes on the other side of the dusty main street of Hope Town. The men were pushing and shoving in a tight circle, heads down, kicking at something on the ground. From the all yelling and the shooting in the air that was going on, Leo guessed the young men were just in off the trail with some longhorns for the stock market that was held every month at Hope Town, and now they were letting off steam, and why not?

Leo had once been on a cattle drive from southern Texas to the railhead, and if he didn't remember the celebrations that followed getting the cattle safely on the railway trucks quite so well as the work, he thought that the spree had been the best part of the experience!

His horse Sunshine, a fine palomino, had drawn level with the cowpokes now. Smiling at some of the memories their high spirits evoked, he glanced across at them as he passed. And then he felt as if he'd been punched in the gut. Lying in the dust between the legs of the men was a tiny huddled figure dressed in blue. A figure with waist-length black hair tumbling about her. They'd got a woman down on the ground. A Mexican or an Indian from the texture and the colour of the hair. Leo slid off his horse and moved towards the yelling men with a stride that never faltered.

'That's enough now.'

Those nearest to him stopped at once and turned to face him. Leo sized up the expressions on the drunken faces. Unshaved, red-eyed, the lads hadn't bothered about cleaning up before hitting the town. They looked rough. They looked dangerous. And a rapid count came up with no fewer than twelve of them. But there was the tiny sprawled figure in the dirt to drive Leo on.

'This ain't sporting, and I guess you all know

it. Why don't you move on down to Madam Bella's where the girls are ready for a bit of fun?'

A couple of the cowpokes laughed out loud. All the rest grinned.

'What? You think you're playing the gentleman? Rescuing a pretty girl?'

'Can't tell if she's pretty,' Leo said calmly, 'but I guess that's what I'm doing.'

His reply provoked howls of laughter. The laughter sounded wrong. Leo looked from one face to another, trying to read their eyes. There was something about the situation he couldn't understand. The ringleader put one hand on his waist and flapped the other hand in the air as he addressed his companions.

'Well, now, he fancies our little treasure. What price the big strong cowboy?'

His cronies thought his remark was hilarious. They laughed, they minced, they cut capers on the dusty street, but it wasn't until one of them stuck out the toe of his boot and rolled over the unconscious figure that Leo realized what they were finding so funny. He was looking down at the bruised and bloodied face of a Chinaman.

Beating or not, outnumbered or not, Leo probably wouldn't have initially gotten involved for a man's sake, but he was in the middle of the situation now, and he would have to handle it. He shook his head and looked rueful.

'There'll be trouble all the same if you kill him.'

One of the cowpokes bristled and dropped his hands so that they hovered within reach of his gun.

'Who cares about a Chink?'

Leo's own hands dropped as well, floating over the handle of the Navy Colt he wore night and day. Tension sparked between the two men.

The ringleader of the cowpokes stepped up and put out a restraining hand.

'Leave it, Hank.'

Another voice rose in agreement.

'Let's go to Madam Bella's. It's girls we want, not little runty Chinamen.'

And the danger was over. The men moved away down the street towards Bella's, laughing and joshing, one of them pretending to mince. Leo's brows snapped together, but he decided not to go after him. Insults were unlikely to find much of an ear in a town where everyone knew him.

'Leo Denver, you're crazier than a rattle-snake.'

Leo whirled to face the speaker, a large, soft-looking man whose waistcoat spread tightly over a large soft belly and who had a cigar in his soft white hands. Leo couldn't help laughing.

'Sheriff Wicks. To the rescue with your usual impeccable timing.'

The soft cheeks flushed.

'You want to watch that mouth of yours, Denver. I came as soon as I heard there was a disturbance.'

Leo said nothing. Everyone knew the sheriff was pusillanimous. But he had his uses. Leo nodded down at the Chinaman.

'Well now you're here, you can take care of him.'

But the sheriff had other ideas.

'You out of your mind? What in tarnation would I do with a Chinaman?'

'Put him in jail,' Leo suggested.

'And waste the town's folks' money?'

It was hot, standing out in the street. Sweat stung Leo's eyes.

'Can't leave him here,' he countered.

The sheriff's gaze surveyed the ground. Spread open in the dust was a battered bag made out of canvas with leather handles. It was empty. A few fragments that the thieves had thought worthless or had overlooked lay in the dirt. A wooden comb, a cooking-pot and a few sheets of paper fluttering in the wind. Leo gathered them up. Then he looked at Sheriff Wicks again. The sheriff's eyes were hard.

'If that Chink's got no money, then he's a vagrant, and I'm entitled to run him out of town.'

Leo didn't trouble to hide the scorn in his voice.

'Mighty public-spirited of you, Wicks.'

The sheriff flushed again.

'That's the law,' he muttered, and hurried away down the street as if he was afraid of what Leo might say next.

Leo shouted after him.

'Wicks, you're a useless windbag!'

Then Leo looked down at the battered figure that still sprawled unconscious at his feet and scratched his head.

'I think he's sick, Leo,' came a voice behind him. 'That Chinkie just about fell off the stage-coach when he arrived here and the driver wouldn't take him no further. Said he might be infectious.'

Every small town has a man like Willy Sticks. Too crippled to work - and the tale of how his

legs lost their use was different at every telling -
he employed himself with odd jobs, drink, gossip
and hanging around. Propelling himself with
the sticks that gave him his name, Willy came
over to Leo now. The two men looked down at
the Chinaman.

'He looks awful sick,' Willy observed. 'I reckon
he'll be a customer for one of Fats' boxes by the
morning.'

Leo hesitated. He didn't want to get any more
involved, but it seemed wrong to walk away, leaving the Chinaman to die in the street. Willy was
thinking.

'Vagrants don't get boxes,' he amended. 'Fats
pops them in a special hole. Plip, plop, they all
go in together, being as how there's no one to
pay for the funeral.'

Leo made up his mind. He walked across the
street to his horse. Sunshine was waiting in the
exact spot where he'd dropped the reins. He led
the mare back. In the few seconds he'd been
turned away, Willy Sticks had bent over the
unconscious Chinaman like a vulture.

'Get your hands off him,' Leo ordered.

'There's nothing in his pockets,' Willy replied,
straightening up with difficulty because of his
disability. 'They rolled him good. Hey, Leo, what

are you doing?'

'I'm taking him to Doc Halliday's.'

'What in thunder for? He'll be dead in a few hours.'

'I wouldn't leave a dog to die out in the street like this.'

Leo lifted the Chinaman, slung him face down across the saddle and tipped his hat to Willy, gathering up the reins to move along, but Willy Sticks had one more piece of news for him.

'Doc Halliday got shot on Thursday and there ain't no new sawbones yet.'

More bad luck! Leo stood in the hot street for a second, wishing more than ever that he'd never gotten involved, but he knew it would kill the Chinaman to abandon him. Sighing, Leo swung himself up into the saddle behind his burden and turned the palomino's head for home.

Sunshine was carrying double load and a month's stores, so he rode at an easy pace. The fierceness had gone out of the sun and the cactus shadows were long before he came in sight of his homestead, the Lucky LD.

Leo was deprecating about his land when he was talking to men like Jake Brody, who ran his beef on better than 1,000 square miles of well-watered land. Saying too much about a quarter section of 160 acres was akin to an Englishman boasting that he had an allotment. But small as it was, Leo was deeply attached to his dust and his rocks and his acres of scrub.

He'd had the place going on eight years now, and the bank manager was starting to concede that making Leo a loan for all that was needed to ranch the place hadn't been that crazy after all. Leo's neighbour to the south, Dai Williams, was a good man and between them they'd set up some neat irrigation systems so that Leo was carrying more than twice the head of cattle he'd had the year before.

As he drew closer to home he saw that a buggy stood in the shade of the barn and that the veranda was graced by two female figures. A large stout one in purple, and a deliciously curved one in pink. Bess, his dog, smelt her master and ran out to bark a welcome. The pink figure jumped to her feet and waved frantically.

Leo's heart jumped like a salmon in his chest and then began to beat far more rapidly than it had when he'd been outfacing twelve drunken men. It was like a sweet dream come true to see

Rose Prescott waiting to greet him after a hard day's work, but in his day-dreams he'd never been so dirty, or so dusty, or carrying an unconscious Chinaman slung over his saddle. Rose's eyes went directly to his burden. Her blue eyes narrowed in suspicion.

'Who's she?' she demanded.

'He, it's a he. And I don't know.'

Rose's delicious mouth wrinkled in disgust.

'Horrid! Oh, Leo! I so need to talk to you!'

He couldn't help hoping. Just a little. He'd loved Rose since he could remember, but her mama didn't consider him eligible. It was surprising that she'd brought her daughter to see him now. It hurt him to turn away from Rose's fragrant and utterly desirable female form, but never in his life had Leo left a horse out in the sun and unwatered when he didn't have to, and there was the Chinaman to unload as well. Rose didn't like the delay.

'I want to talk to you! Leave the horse! Leave that man!'

'Might as well put him on the sofa now as later.'

Leo wondered if Rose might know anything about nursing. Out West, a lot of women became pretty handy at dealing with the sick. But she took one look at his burden and turned away in disgust.

'Ugh! Put him in the barn! You might catch something vile!'

'Bug bites me, the bug dies,' Leo said, moving past her into the cabin.

Inside the simple one-roomed cabin, he hesitated for a moment and then laid the Chinaman on the single bed. Then he pulled off the little man's funny split-toed canvas boots and tried to give the unconscious form a drink of water. Most of it trickled out from the lax lips and went on the pillow, but Leo was aware of Rose waiting for him outside and decided that would have to do. He washed his hands and went back out to see to Sunshine. Then, at last, he was free to be with Rose.

She had taken off her bonnet and was decoratively draped against one of the veranda posts, golden hair floating to her waist. Leo's breath caught in his throat at the sight of her. He moved towards her, knowing that his heart was in his eyes.

'Rose, you have to be the most beautiful girl in the world.'

She came closer to him in a rustle of pink petticoats. Her blue, blue eyes met his directly, and he saw a soft tear welling up and then spilling down her perfect skin.

'It's so terrible that I don't know how to tell you!'

'I'll kill anyone who upsets you! Tell me who and I'll kill them for you.'

'Darling Leo! But there's nothing you can do! You know how we are situated! Poor Mamma alone with thirteen children to raise! I had hoped, Leo, that you and I . . . but it cannot be! And I have come here to ask you not to think of me any more!'

Well, he'd known, hadn't he? He felt a nerve jumping in his clenched jaw.

'Who is it?'

'Jake Brody has done me the honour of asking me to be his wife!'

He'd known that as well. Who else but the bull-headed Jake Brody with his cigars and his cattle and his money in the bank?

'You'll look swell in that fancy house of his, Rose.'

'He's promised to look after Mamma, Leo! And all the little ones as well!'

Just for a second he let her see what he was feeling.

'Rose, don't you see I can't stand it?'

'Time's up, sweetie!' called her Mamma.

'Oh, Mamma! Just a few minutes more!'

'No,' Leo said brusquely. 'There's no more to say. I wish you very happy, Rose. Servant, Mrs Prescott.'

And he strode into his cabin, slamming the door behind him.

CHAPTER TWO

There were plenty of chores to keep Leo busy, but he managed to get back to the cabin in-between tasks to check on the Chinaman, who didn't look good. Leo knew he was no earthly use at nursing, but there was no one else, so he got up a time or two in the night as well. He sponged the little man's hot face and tried to get him to drink, but it seemed to do no good, and by mid-morning the next day his guest was failing.

'Suppose I'll have to bury him next,' Leo muttered to himself, as he went out to see what had set Bess to barking.

A blade-slim girl in a ripped and dusty blue dress ran up the two steps to the veranda and flopped down on the home-made wooden settle. One of Rose's many sisters, he wasn't sure which.

This one had heavy dark brows that slanted over her forehead and stood out on a crimson face.

'I'm so h-hot!'

'I'll get you a dipper of water.'

'Thank you, Leo.'

He fetched her water in a tin cup and she drank the whole lot in unladylike gulps. He looked at her, bewildered.

'You never came all this way without a horse?'

Merry dark eyes met his.

'I f-fell off.'

Leo stirred uneasily.

'Your folks will go plumb crazy when the horse comes back without you.'

A decided shake of the head.

'They won't know. I was r-riding like the Indians do, without a saddle or bridle, and besides, everyone's so busy with the wedding that they'll never miss m-me.'

Leo looked very hard at the ground by his feet.

'Rose getting married today, is she?'

His visitor chuckled.

'She's m-married now. I saw the d-dirty deed done before I left'

His face must have given away more than he would have liked, because Leo heard a new note in his ragamuffin visitor's voice.

'Oh, I'm sorry. I f-forgot for a minute that you were one of Rose's swains. But you know, Primrose is almost as p-pretty. Why not take her?'

'I guess you're too young to know how it works, short stuff,' Leo replied. 'But hang on a minute. I thought you were Primrose?'

'No, I'm Jasmine. But will you call me J-Jack instead? Jasmine doesn't suit me.'

'Maybe you'll grow into the name,' he suggested.

She gave a shake of her head that set her dark curls flying.

'It's my seventeenth birthday next month! J-Jasmines don't stammer.'

'I never noticed.'

She cocked her head and regarded him like a small, intelligent sparrow.

'Really?'

He couldn't meet her eyes and lie, so he turned away instead.

'You rest up a minute longer. I'll get the horses ready to take you home.'

'No! I mean t-thank you, but I haven't seen the Chinaman yet.'

'He's sick. I won't let you near him.'

'I'm not afraid of infection.'

'Think I'm gonna let you fetch the fever back to your place?'

He felt her eyes checking his face, reading his expression. Then she gave a sigh.

'No, you're n-not. And it's no good my arguing with you. I can see that.'

'Smart girl.'

Jasmine showed Leo a package about the size of a tobacco wad. 'I bought some Indian medicine for the Chinaman.'

'Indian?'

'An old l-lady visited our place last year. She taught me a lot of useful things.'

'Like how to ride a pony?'

'That was m-mean. She was too old to show me riding!'

Leo regarded the ragamuffin before him. She held out her package trustingly.

'It's bark from willow trees. It w-works, I've used it before.'

Leo took the fabric-tied bundle and tossed it from hand to hand.

'Might kill him.'

'So it might. And so m-might doing nothing.'

Suddenly Leo didn't care any more. Rose Prescott was married, and the Chinaman was the next best thing to dead, anyway.

'What's to lose?'

All the time he was boiling up the medicine,
taking Jasmine home, coming back to give the
Chinaman a second dose, shutting his place
down for the night, Leo fought against the temp-
tation that raged inside him. But in the end he
could stand it no longer. When he went down
the corral Sunshine whickered in her friendly
way and came to meet him. He patted the
palomino's satin-soft nose.

'You don't want to be out with me tonight,
girl.'

He looked around the enclosure at the other
horses and settled on a half-wild black bronco.
It had been gelded late, and wasn't fully
broken, but Leo was in no mood to stand any
nonsense. He roped the beast and wrestled on
the saddle and bridle, and then set out for town
in a mad gallop that did nothing to relieve his
feelings.

The moon was up and nearly full. It shone so
brightly that it was easy to travel fast. Leo could
see every rut and hole in the dusty track that he
was gradually wearing between his place and
town. He whipped the horse on unmercifully. By
the time he got to Madam Bella's hitching-post

22

the bronco was glad to stand quietly, though Leo hobbled him to make sure the beast didn't get ideas about escaping.

Inside Bella's the polished wood and scarlet drapes and tinkling piano didn't bring him the comfort he'd hoped for. He flung a large dollar bill at the barman.

'Leave the bottle out.'

The barman took one look at Leo's face, put out a bottle and a glass without saying a word, and prudently went back to reading the newspaper he had spread out on the end of the bar. Bella's girls were not so tactful. They swarmed around him like mosquitos and Leo had to keep swatting them away. Another soft hand patted his thigh invitingly, Leo lifted his head and growled.

'Can't you-all take no for an answer?'

A rich, seductive perfume curled under his nose.

'Leo Denver, and we was used to be such good friends.'

He looked up and met familiar brown eyes.

'Don't bother me tonight, Bella, there's a good girl.'

Bella regarded Leo with understanding in her eyes and a pitying shake of her glossy curls. She waved a white arm, indicating a scatter of depressed male drinkers around the room.

'Rose Prescott's wedding is so bad for business. You guys should hold a wake.'

Leo sucked at his whiskey and ignored her. But one of the solo drinkers reacted.

'Rose Prescott? Did she turn this place into a morgue?'

Everyone looked at the speaker. A stranger, sitting by the bar a way down from Leo, was tapping his white fingers irritably on the polished surface. The thick white skin of his face was disfigured by sunburn, suggesting that he'd ridden a long distance to reach Hope Town that day. He'd changed into fancy black clothes before hitting the bar. His unnaturally black hair had a greasy shine, his hairy freckled hands resembled the legs of a red spider, and altogether he was about as cute as a slug in a cellar. Quiet night or not, Bella's girls didn't seem keen to approach him. And his sour expression suggested he wasn't having the good night out he'd expected.

'*Forget* Rose Prescott! I'm looking for some action.'

The stranger swung round to yell at the piano-player.

24

'Leave off the death march and play something cheerful!'

The piano player's fingers stumbled a little, then broke into an irritating, bouncy quick-time tune. Leo slid off his barstool.

'You want to watch your mouth when it comes to talking of Rose Prescott.'

A cowboy went over to the piano and objected to the new tune. The music jangled to a halt. The stranger realized that his intention to create a party atmosphere had been frustrated, and he glared at Leo viciously. His eyes were brown and framed by sparse ginger lashes. The man slid off his own barstool - he was tall when he stood up - spat on the floor and faced Leo.

'If you hayseeds don't wanna party then I guess we could do fighting instead.'

A stir ran around the bar. To smash a few chairs and break a few glasses would relieve a lot of men's feelings that night. But Leo wasn't so easily drawn.

'You want to have a care, stranger. You're not in your own town tonight.'

The stranger didn't heed the warning, but spoke with whiskey-fuelled courage.

'I'm not the kind of yellow-belly that can't fight without his pals.'

Bella and her girls, the barman, the piano-player and all the cowboys in the bar pressed closer to see what would happen. Leo looked at the stranger.

'Sit down, shut up and leave us all be, sonny,' Leo advised.

A hot light sprang in the stranger's eyes and his whole body tensed. He drawled his words with deliberate insult.

'Rose Prescott is a two-bit whore and she'll spread her legs for anybody.'

The batwing doors never moved, but at that second death entered the room. The cowboys, who'd have thrown themselves into a good-hearted punch-up, backed off as they felt the dreadful force that filled the room. The piano player slid behind his instrument and used it as a shield and the barman vanished behind the protection of his bar. Bella's girls fluttered and squawked and flew for the outer edges of the room like an aviary full of birds when a panther gets in.

Leo automatically reached for his gun but, like the stranger, he'd had to leave his weapons at the door of the hotel. He sized up his adversary. The man's short body was muscled and his long legs looked powerful. Leo made up his mind and moved all in the same second, throwing a powerful uppercut with his right fist. He aimed at the stranger's right eye, but the man turned his face, so that the blow landed across his jawbone. There was so much power in that punch that it would have felled a lesser man and finished the fight, but although the stranger's head snapped back and he staggered back into the bar, he swiftly caught his balance and whipped around to face Leo once more.

Leo fought to gain his own balance and size up the situation. His knuckles were screaming where they'd delivered the blow to the stranger's jaw and hot liquid ran down his belly. He'd felt no pain, but his shirt was split down the centre and was rapidly turning red. Now, too late, he saw silver glinting in the stranger's dead-white hand.

'Knife!' shouted one of the cowboys.

'Look out, Leo!' screamed Bella at the same time.

Leo fell into a crouch and made a wary half-circle around the man, looking for an opening, moving first to the left and then back to the right and then to the left again. The stranger kept his back to the bar and circled at the same speed as Leo, keeping the knife between them, using it as

27

a shield, certain in his own mind that no man would be crazy enough to rush onto that wicked blade. The stranger flipped back his pitch-black hair and laughed out loud. His hot brown eyes were scornful.

'Rose Prescott might be married but her husband can't be watching over her all the time. Why buy the cow when you can have milk for nothing? You should be celebrating. You can have that whore anytime. She's willing—'

Leo sprang. He felt a sharp pricking thump in the top of his thigh, and he knew that the knife had gone in, but he had both hands wrapped around the throat of stranger and he had no mind to let go, whatever the damage to his own person might be. The stranger's eyes rolled back in his head, his knees went limp and he seemed to fold down towards the floor. He knocked back into his stool, which spun and fell over, clattering on the planks as it rolled.

Leo followed the stranger down to the dirty wooden floor of the bar, never letting go of his grip on the man's corpse-white throat. In fact he dug in his thumbs deeper as a vicious satisfaction flooded his being. He was kneeling now, bent so close over the stranger that he could smell the man's greasy personal scent, see the freckles that stood out in the freaky white skin. The smell of fear-soaked sweat was so strong that Leo's stomach retched in protest, but nothing would have made him let go.

The man's boot-heels drummed on the wooden floor as he struggled for his life. Leo knew it took longer than you'd think to actually finish a man, and he held on while the stranger's dead-white face suffused with mottled red, and he held on while the tongue lolled out of the mouth in a disgusting trail of spittle and turned black, and he still held on while the kicking boot-heels faded from a frantic tattoo to a few feeble kicks to a terrifying stillness. Blood from Leo's gashed stomach poured over them both, turning the world red. Leo could hear voices yelling at him overhead to quit. He was aware of Bella, braver than most, actually pulling on his arms and screaming in his ear.

'Leo! You gotta stop that now! You're killing him!'

And now, at last, Leo felt an unmistakable change in the stranger's body as death claimed his prize. The man's spirit left the room. Leo finally let go, the limp body fell the last few inches to the ground and lay horribly still. Leo rocked back on his heels and looked up at Bella.

'I gave him every chance to walk away.'

Her brown eyes were anxious.

'Here comes the sheriff. Sheriff Wicks, I can testify. It was self-defence. The stranger had a knife. . . .'

Handcuffs gleamed between Sheriff Wicks's soft hands.

'Who threw the first punch?'

Silence. Deep, uncomfortable silence.

And the cuffs snapped over Leo's wrists before he even understood the danger he was in. The sheriff's eyes held a sly, triumphant gleam and as Leo scanned them he realized what an enemy he'd made yesterday. The sheriff's words confirmed that he was avenging what he saw as Leo's insults.

'As a public-spirited man, it's my duty to take you into custody.'

And five minutes later, the iron bars of the town jail clanged shut behind Leo.

CHAPTER THREE

It was impossible to break out of the town jail. Leo knew that because he'd helped design and build it. The wooden-frame building held three cells made out of iron bars, each cell at a good distance from the others, and each a good distance again from the wooden walls. The cell area was connected to the front part of the office by a corridor-cum-storeroom. In front of that Sheriff Wicks dozed behind a wooden counter or slumped on the porch and watched the world go by.

Leo lay on the bare concrete floor of his cell and thought grimly that when he'd convinced the committee that they should allow the prisoners a tiny window in the wooden frame of the building - heavily barred and at a safe distance from the cells - it had never entered his head that he might be one of the poor souls benefiting from the meagre slice of light and air. He heard keys rattling and two voices whispering along the corridor. A heavenly aroma of coffee, bacon and beans filled the air.

'Hey, Leo, you awake?' one of the voices demanded.

Leo had to work hard at not wincing as he got to his feet from the cold concrete.

'Tom,' he greeted the deputy.

The deputy unlocked the door of a small grille low in the front of the cell and pushed in the tray of food.

'Looks good!' Leo ejaculated in surprise.

He didn't remember the town taking any decisions to feed prisoners royally. But then he saw that the second whisperer was Benny, the natural who skivvied for Mrs Bentley's boarding-house and café. Benny beamed at Leo now.

'Miss Prescott said I was to feed you well.'

Leo felt a flame of gladness in his heart.

'Rose? She's thinking of me?'

Benny's moon face was still lit with his silly smile.

'Rose wouldn't give you the snot from her handkerchief. No, it's Miss Jasmine what paid me to feed you.'

Tom the deputy grabbed the natural's shirt collar and dragged him up the passageway. Benny yelped.

'But Tom, you know it's true. It was you as said she was marrying a midden for its muck and you said—'

A box on the ear interrupted Benny's words as Tom hissed at him.

'Don't you know that Leo Denver is in jail for killing a man for insulting Rose Prescott? Lord have mercy on you, Benny, 'cos you sure ain't got no sense.'

When he came back Tom kept a nervous distance from the bars of the cell.

'Don't mind Benny none, Mr Denver. He's the way the Lord made him.'

'Tom, you know me better than that.'

The deputy's face cleared some.

'Strange times, Leo. I never thought to see you in here,' he apologized. 'I don't hardly know how to take it.'

The smell of his breakfast could be resisted no longer. Leo reached for the tin cup. Coffee had never tasted so good.

'Thank Miss Jasmine for me, Tom.'

'She wanted to come and visit you, but of

course I wouldn't let her. She said she's sorting the cattle and Sunshine and she's looking after your Chinaman.'

'Tell her not to bother,' Leo said grimly.

The full horror of his plight came over him. He was as helpless as a new-born babe. If a sixteen-year-old girl chose to meddle in his affairs there was nothing he could do to stop her.

'Tom, when's the circuit judge due?' he demanded. 'I got to get out of here.'

Tom's unease returned, and he could no longer look Leo in the eye.

'I wouldn't bet on it, Leo. Sheriff seems determined to hang you.'

'Forget Wicks, he's loco. I'll get out. Tom, I need to clean these knife gashes.'

But Sheriff Wicks was walking towards them and he had overheard.

'Well, ain't it a shame. Hope Town's new doctor won't be here 'til next month.'

The deputy was more charitable.

'Whiskey cleans cuts. I'll get you some.'

Sheriff Wicks wasn't pleased.

'Tom, I forbid you to waste whiskey on him. Denver don't need that leg of his anyhow. He won't be walking no further than the scaffold after the judge hears what I have to tell him on Wednesday.'

Leo turned away and concentrated on his breakfast. Sheriff Wicks hung around with an irritating grin on his face, but when he realized that he couldn't make Leo acknowledge any of his stupid remarks he gave up and went away. Later that day Tom slipped down the passage bearing a bottle.

'Illegal moonshine,' he whispered. 'To clean your cuts with, Leo. Don't drink it. It'll send you blind.'

'I won't need to see anything if the sheriff has his way.'

The cut across Leo's belly was shallow and had stopped bleeding. He sloshed moonshine over the gash, holding his breath as the icy liquid hit and then blazed into fire. The wound in his upper thigh was deep and still oozing. Leo didn't think the knife had hit anything vital. Although it was painful, he seemed to be able to move the leg all right. The biggest danger was infection, so he ignored the agony and trickled moonshine into the swollen red hole until he was sure the whole area was treated.

The enforced rest of the next few days was probably the best treatment for Leo's knife wounds, but it did his mental state no good. He spent the first day lying on the concrete floor. He was glad when Dai Williams came to see him, and brought in a horse blanket. Shock was evident in his neighbour's eyes.

'It's a blow to see you in jail. I can't believe they'll hang you.'

Leo knew what the man wanted.

'You'll be thinking about the irrigation system,' he suggested.

'Look, I wouldn't have mentioned it. But Leo, my systems won't work without the main artesian feed, and that's on your land.'

'I owe my soul to the bank,' Leo said. 'You know that, Dai. But if you ask the lawyer to come see me, we can arrange for you to take over my loans.'

'That's generous of you, Leo. But have you no kin of your own whatever?'

'None but a God-bothering brother, and we ain't speaking.'

'Look, let me write him a letter for you.'

'No thanks, Dai. Send in the lawyer and I'll see you get the land.'

Dai looked disconsolate.

'Johnson the lawyer ran off with Ted Peebles' wife last night. Ted's gone after them with a gun, so I don't think the lawyer'll be back in Hope Town.'

'Get me some paper to write my will. We'll have the bank-manager act witness.'

Dai looked at the ground uncomfortably and twisted his hands together.

'That's mighty civil of you, Leo. And, look, if there was anything I could do. . . .'

'Thanks for the blanket,' Leo said, and Dai made his escape thankfully.

Leo had a good number of these awkward visits. His friends and neighbours were shocked, wished they could do something, but. . . .

The rest of the time Leo spent sprawled on his blanket. Some of the time his mind ranged backwards, wishing that his mother had lived longer so that he could remember more of her than the rustle of blue skirts and a sense of gentleness. Sometimes he thought of escaping, but there seemed to be no way out.

It wasn't until Tuesday afternoon that he heard the bray of an indignant donkey right outside the wood of the jailhouse. Then he heard feet kicking at the walls, and eventually a woman's face appeared at the slot of the barred window. The head blocked the light, but he could see slanting dark eyebrows, and a

37

mass of tumbling curls.

'Jasmine! What in thunder are you doing?'

'Standing on a d-donkey to reach the window. They wouldn't l-let me in.'

'I should think not! Jail is no place for a lady.'

'Then I'm glad I'm n-not a lady!'

He laughed out loud, and so did she. It was a good sound in a bad place.

'Sunshine is fine and so is Bess, and so are all your c-cattle. My brother Nathan is minding them for you. He wants to be a rancher, you know.'

Leo was distracted by the sound of glass smashing and splintering up the street.

'What's that?'

Jasmine's face disappeared and then came back.

'A drunk got thrown out of Bella's by the bounty hunter who rode in yesterday looking for Red Murdo the bank robber.'

'Red Murdo!' Luke said. 'Red!'

An image of a man with unnaturally black hair, thick white skin and sparse ginger lashes popped into his mind. Hope rose in him like a trumpet blast.

'Jasmine,' he said urgently, 'did Lawyer Johnson come back to town?'

'Ted Peebles shot him.'

Leo punched his fist into the palm of his hand in exasperation. Dang! It was hard to do business in a town where the key players insisted on getting themselves shot every six months! He'd have to ask his neighbour.

'Jasmine, I need you to get a message out to Dai Williams. It's urgent!'

But she wouldn't go until he told her why. Her intelligent little face screwed up like a monkey's as she worked out the implications of Leo's suspicions.

'You want Dai to ask the bounty hunter what Red Murdo looked like, and take the bounty hunter over to Fats the undertaker to see if the b-body can be identified?'

'Hurry up or they'll have buried him!'

'If they have, I'll make them d-dig up the corpse.'

Her face vanished from the window. Leo listened to her geeing up the donkey. It was bitter to have a girl acting as his champion. It was hard to wait, knowing that his life depended on her. Leo was awake all night, tense with frustration and optimism and expectation, turning restlessly on Dai's old horse blanket.

'I'll get out of here and I'll get even with

Wicks, I swear it.'

But the next morning, when he heard feet coming down the passageway and keys clinking, Leo couldn't guess whether he was going to be a free man or taken to a fixed trial with a swing on a rope at the end.

CHAPTER FOUR

Leo tried to keep his voice calm as he looked up at the deputy sheriff.

'Come to hang me, Tom?'

The deputy swung open the jail cell door.

'We'll leave that to the devil. You must have cut a deal with him to get so lucky.'

Leo walked out into main street of humdrum old Hope Town and for a few special moments revelled in being free and alive. Then a man in a dark suit who had been standing in the shade of the bank opposite the jail walked across the street and spoke to him.

'That leg of yours looks mighty stiff.'

Leo looked into self-possessed green eyes. The stranger wore a smart dark suit and a dandified if old-fashioned neckcloth. His taste in guns was old-fashioned as well. He was carrying a Plains rifle and the pistol at his belt was a Cherokee.

'You're the bounty hunter?' Leo guessed.

A cool tip of the hat.

'John O'Connor at your service.'

'It was Red Murdo, then?'

When he smiled, John O'Connor was a like-able-looking man.

'I was well on my way to California when that little girl of yours comes tearing after me like an Apache.'

Leo felt a surge of anger. He'd told her to fetch Dai. The bounty hunter seemed to read his expression.

'Hold your horses now. What else could she be doing? I was well on my way, and I'd have missed my chance at Red Murdo and a five-thousand-dollar bounty.'

Suddenly Leo realized what the man was after.

'You're welcome to it.'

Cool green eyes scanned his face.

'It's a deal of money. You might be regretting it later.'

Leo simply shrugged.

'Shall we step across to the bank?'

The bank was empty when they walked in. Clarence Carnegie, the bank-manager, flapped and dithered like a funny old hen.

'Bounty, well, I don't know if I'm authorized to pay out a bounty. I'm sure we've never had a bounty hunter in Hope before.'

The bank door banged. A couple of men walked in and pretended to wait in line behind Leo and the bounty hunter. Really they were listening to every word.

Leo gripped the bank-manager by the shoulders and turned him so that he faced a handbill that was stuck to the wall. The handbill offered: *$5000 reward for Red Murdo, dead or alive.*

'There's your authorization,' Leo suggested.

Mr Carnegie swallowed hard.

'I don't know. . . .'

John O'Connor's green eyes were like flint.

'If you want more authorization, I'll fetch you the corpse of Red Murdo.'

Mr Carnegie's cheeks went white. Jim Brady, the clerk, had a lame leg from polio which meant that he had to get his living in the bank, but he was full of spirit.

'I've already seen the corpse, Mr Carnegie, sir. I was at Fats the undertaker's when Mr O'Connor here made the identification. None of us had no doubts, but Sheriff Wicks was awful sorry to believe it. He sure wanted to hang you, Leo. We had to strip the corpse and look at the hair on its privates before the sheriff would accept that the man was a natural redhead.'

'That will do, Brady,' snapped Carnegie.

The door opened again and two ladies came in, followed by a crowd of men and Willy Sticks, who had suddenly found an errand at the bank. Thirty pairs of eyes watched Mr Carnegie count out $5,000 in new bills and deposit them in front of John O'Connor. The bounty hunter gestured at Leo to take the money.

'You killed the man.'

'You identified him. You take it.'

Mr Carnegie was scandalized.

'Denver! Think of your repayments. You can't afford to turn down any part of five thousand dollars if you want that new water-pump you've been talking about.'

Leo grinned and looked at the bounty hunter.

'You saved my neck, you know. You're welcome to the money.'

John O'Connor took the money, counted it far faster than Mr Carnegie had done, then peeled off 1,000 of the dollars. He pushed them at the bank-manager.

'Pay this off my friend's account.'

A satisfied stir ran around the watching towns-folk.

'Spoken like a gentleman, sir,' said Grandpa Watkins.

John O'Connor tipped his hat and gave Leo another amused glance.

'Shall we leave?'

The man's stylish gesture had made it impossible to argue further, so Leo walked out of the bank with the bounty hunter and then bade him goodbye with a feeling of regret. In other circumstances the two men could have been friends. It seemed that John O'Connor felt it too.

'I'm still in your debt by a long way,' he told Leo, and his green eyes were friendly. 'Here's me with the bounty and you with the knife marks. If John O'Connor can do you a favour anytime, you need only say the word.'

Leo watched the man ride away until he was out of sight before turning to the problem of his own transport. He decided go to the stagecoach office and hire or buy a horse, but when he walked into the stables he was greeted by Sam Turner the groom.

'Nice to see you, Leo. Your bill is paid up to today, as it happens.'

Sam led out the black bronco and saddled and bridled it while Leo stood by, not daring to say a word lest he exploded. More of Jasmine Prescott's meddling! Why it made him so mad to have her solve his problems was a question he didn't address.

Partly because of his injured leg Leo rode back to the Lucky LD at a much slower pace than he'd ridden out a week ago. The black bronco went well. The wild ride seemed to have mended its manners. Leo knew he was lucky to be riding the trail to his home. A hawk circled lazily in the deep blue of the sky. Lizards scurried in the dust as his shadow fell over them. A cactus bore vivid pink blossoms that hadn't been there a week ago. He could have lost it all, thanks to Wicks.

As he drew closer to his cabin Bess came tearing out, barking a welcome. Leo was surprised to see smoke rising from the chimney.

'That meddling girl better not be in my cabin,' Leo told the bronco while he rubbed him down. Then he turned the horse out.

But of course she was. And so was the Chinaman.

'I'd plumb forgotten about you,' Leo blurted, too surprised to be tactful.

The Chinaman bowed.

'I guess you had more important things on

your mind,' he suggested in excellent English.

His accent was crystal clear, and unmistakably American. Leo stared into the slanting black eyes and tried to size the man up. His face was thin, and bore traces of bruising from his beating as well as the shadows of his illness. but he was plainly over his fever.

'You look better.'

The Chinaman bowed again.

'Thanks to your excellent care. Seventh Chinese Son most obliged.'

Jasmine butted in.

'Only I c-call him Charlie, because we can't say Seventh Chinese Son every time. Just think, Leo, his p-parents had so many children that they never had time to think of a name for poor C-Charlie.'

Leo gave her a quelling look. Her slanting black brows lifted in hurt surprise.

'Charlie's got the most exciting story to tell you, Leo - all about g-gold. He's got a m-map. All in Chinese so no one can read it.'

Leo lifted one hand.

'Later. Right now I want to check my stock.'

The Chinaman simply bowed again, his air as calm as a summer's day. Jasmine was boiling with impatience, but Leo paid her no mind until he'd visited Sunshine, been around the barn and the corral, checked out those steers that he'd branded two weeks ago and made sure the irrigation was running as it should be. To his surprise, the Lucky LD was in apple-pie order despite his week away. Then Leo heard a cough that was meant to make him aware of a lanky boy who was hovering nervously in the doorway of the barn. The lad was about fourteen years old. He had a round freckled face and a thick fringe of brown hair falling into shy brown eyes. Leo smiled at him.

'You Jasmine's brother?'

'Yes, sir. I'm Nathan, sir.'

'If this here's your doing then I have to thank you.'

The lad's eyes shone and a pleased flush rose to his cheeks.

'I like doing it, sir. I want to be a rancher.'

'I'm glad to have you here.'

Leo was rewarded by a grateful expression and a shy smile. They finished up the evening chores together, and Leo found himself heading up to the cabin well before his usual time.

'It's good to have help,' he said half to himself.

He found that it was good to have company in

the house as well. The cabin was scrubbed and spotless and even the cooker he'd made out of old oil-cans was polished until it shone. The Chinaman's funny-shaped cooking-pot sat on the flames and an appetizing smell hung in the air. There were flowers on the table, so Leo went out again to tip a dipper of water over his head and Nathan went with him to the pump.

'Women!' said Leo with feeling.

And Nathan gave him a sympathetic grin.

They went back in and Leo said grace, feeling strange because it was the first time he'd ever headed his own table with more than one sitting at it. He sniffed at his food cautiously to start with. It was all tiny bits and pieces cut up in some kind of sauce, but after the first bite he was happy to wade in.

'Charlie's just the best c-cook in the world,' said Jasmine.

'Want a job?' agreed Leo.

The Chinaman managed a polite bow despite the fact that he was sitting down, holding wooden chopsticks and eating.

'Tell Leo about the gold,' Jasmine chanted impatiently.

The Chinaman sketched designs in the air with his chopsticks while he talked.

'I live in New York. All the Tang family live in New York. We have a restaurant. We have a laundry. My uncle has a bank. Very good business all round. But my brother, Third Chinese Son, Dragon of Prosperity, he wanted more. He wanted adventure. So, he went to California and he registered a gold claim.'

'Like thousands before him,' Leo said. 'Most break their hearts.'

The Chinaman's slanting black eyes sparkled with glee.

'Only this time the fairy-tale came true. My brother found gold. He found lots and lots of gold. He hid most of it and brought home all he could carry.'

The Chinaman turned away for a second, seemed to adjust his blue robes, then turned back and a sparkling nugget of gold appeared on the table. Leo picked it up.

'It's heavy for its size,' he marvelled.

Charlie nodded.

'Gold is weighty. My brother couldn't carry it back to New York. The family sent me to fetch it, but alone I soon got into trouble. Will you come with me to California? I'll split the gold with you.'

Leo felt the siren call of adventure, he couldn't deny it.

'But my stock. . . .' he mused.

Nathan sat up and spoke with the painful shyness of the adolescent.

'Sir, I'd mind your cattle for you. I'd do it real well, if you could trust me.'

Jasmine quickly collected the dishes and cleared the table. She gave the wooden planks a swift wipe down, then Charlie spread out the papers that Leo had rescued. Leo could understand the documents that were in English: printed maps, claim documents, assay reports on the quality of the gold, and a bank statement that made his eyebrows rise. It all looked convincing enough. But then there was a map covered in spidery Chinese writing. Leo frowned at it crossly.

'How can anyone make head or tail of this lot?' he demanded.

Charlie fetched the slate Leo used for his shopping list and squiggled on it in chalk. He slid the resulting drawing under Leo's nose.

'What does that look like?'

Leo squinted.

'A pine tree?' he guessed, only half serious.

'You're a smart guy. It's a tree. Now, three wavy lines, think of water running.'

'A river?'

'You are very smart.'

The chalk moved again. This time Charlie drew the jagged outline of some mountain-tops, then he simplified the drawing into a Chinese character.

'And that one means mountain,' Leo said in wonder, understanding.

Leo picked up the map and studied the Chinese writing again. He was able to pick out the three characters he recognized.

'Is that all there is to it?'

'Simple.'

Jasmine drew her heavy brows together.

'Charlie,' she asked suspiciously, 'How many of these s-symbols are there?'

'Around forty thousand. But three thousand characters are enough for every day.'

Leo pushed the map and the slate away from him.

'And twenty-five years to learn it. I don't think I'll bother.'

'I'll translate the map for you,' Charlie offered.

'No. Keep it to yourself. Charlie.'

Jasmine reached for the map and pored over it.

'What's this s-symbol at the top mean, Charlie?'

'The most important one,' Charlie replied, smiling. 'Gold.'

Jasmine fairly bounced in her chair.

'Leo, when will you s-set off?'

'I ain't said I'm going.'

'But you must! Think what you can do with all that g-gold.'

'Needs thinking about. Charlie, what about

your brother? Won't he have something to say if you share your gold with a stranger?'

'My brother got sick and died. That's why my family sent me. I'm no good at adventure. If you come with me I can stay alive and still keep half of the treasure.'

'Let's sleep on it,' Leo said.

He looked at Jasmine and Nathan, holding their gaze seriously.

'Keep this quiet. People would kill for that map.'

They nodded.

'Charlie, put your papers and this nugget away. You must have a good place. Those cowpokes missed quite a hoard when they rolled you.'

Charlie's eyes twinkled.

'I'll keep them safe until morning,' he agreed. 'Then we'll talk more.'

Jasmine jumped to her feet and put on her cloak. Nathan got up too, but he hung around by the door, wringing his hands.

'Sir, would you mind . . . I mean . . . I'd sure be happy if I could. . . .'

'Nathan, I'd like it fine if you come and help me with the chores tomorrow.'

The lad beamed as if Leo had given him a

present. Leo watched the two Prescotts ride towards their ranch, then he went back inside to find that Charlie had cleared up from the meal and was ready to turn in. The Chinaman bedded down on the home-made settle so Leo had his own bed back. But he didn't sleep any better that night than he had on the floor of the cell. He had too much to think about. Was he justified in leaving his stock on what could be a fool's errand? Could he afford to turn down what might be his only chance to pay off his loans and maybe even buy enough land to be a serious rancher?

When at last he fell asleep he was dreaming of land. Land that stretched out as far as the eye could see and all of it his, free and clear.

CHAPTER FIVE

When Leo woke at dawn the next morning his mind was made up. A man could spend his whole life struggling and never get his head beyond his bank loans. Wild as the scheme sounded, it was his only chance to get rich. He'd go to California. When he told Charlie his decision the Chinaman smiled and made a second, even larger, gold nugget appear beside the first one.

'Get stagecoach tickets,' he suggested. 'You'll be fit to travel by next week.'

'I'm fit now,' growled Leo.

Charlie glanced at Leo's injured leg.

'Maybe I still have some fever. Get tickets for next week.'

It wasn't worth arguing until he knew on what

days the stagecoach travelled. Leo went outside to check on Nathan. He had to show him a few things, but the lad was shaping up well. After lunch he went to the corral. Sunshine came over to meet him in her usual friendly manner, and this time he didn't reject her. Leo whistled softly as he groomed the palomino and then put on her saddle and bridle.

'Come on, girl. We got business in town today.'

Clarence Carnegie showed no surprise when Leo plonked two enormous nuggets of pure gold on the bank counter.

'Ah! The gold that the Chinaman brought back from California.'

Leo nearly fell over with the shock. It was a tremendous effort to say nothing. His mind raced while he watched Carnegie weighing and fussing with the gold. How in the world had the news reached town? So far as Leo knew, only he, Nathan and Jasmine knew the Chinaman's story. The number of dollar bills that Mr Carnegie proposed to exchange for the nuggets was another shock. Leo knew he'd never reach home without some local blood relieving him of such a tempting sum. So Leo kept $2,000 - more cash than he'd ever carried loose in his life - and put the rest in his account. Despite his unease that the story was out, Leo went on to the stagecoach depot to enquire about tickets to California.

'Now then, Leo,' said Buck Harper, who ran the transport side of the business. 'You'll be off to San Diego, no doubt, to pick up that Chinaman's gold?'

'Small towns!' Leo said bitterly. 'A man's business should be his own.'

'Shall I reserve you two seats for Saturday next? If you go by Wednesday's stage it travels via Snakebend and Gulch Creek, so you don't get there no quicker than leaving on Saturday anyway.'

As Leo paid for the tickets that Buck had suggested he realized that there was a man pretending to talk horses with Sam Turner and another slinking around the corner of the stable with Willy Sticks. Leo could feel eyes on his back as he walked to the general store. Ben Williams came running to meet him.

'Howdy, Leo! Are you going to stock up for your expedition to California? Will you be buying a mule? I got shovels on sale and all.'

'It's too far to ride. I got stagecoach tickets. I called in to pick up my usual order, is all.'

Ben threw Leo's groceries into a sack, talking excitedly the whole time.

'I often thought of taking a flutter on the goldfields myself. There sure ain't no profit in storekeeping. You want a hand? I'd give up this place in a minute.'

'Thanks, but no thanks. Better double the food order because I got the Chinaman back at my place, and young Nathan Prescott as well.'

'Seems to me I'd better treble it.'

Ben had beautifully solved the problem of how Leo could order extra supplies without raising suspicions. Leo had already decided that if he and the Chinaman didn't hit the trail that night they might as well forget the gold. But he wanted the watchers to think he was taking the stagecoach for as long as possible.

Ben said: 'Shame I can't rent you a donkey to carry all this stuff. Only my one was stolen last Tuesday and I ain't had time to find another.'

Leo gulped as he realized that he knew the horse-thief, but he managed to speak calmly.

'My mare'll manage the extra load, thanks Ben. Good day to you.'

Ben came to the store door with him and called after Leo down the street.

'Good luck to you in California! Bring back

lots of gold!'

There was no point getting mad at Ben and his mouth. The watchers knew all about the gold. Leo could feel eyes on him all the way to the outskirts of town, but he didn't think he was followed on the way back to the Lucky LD.

'But I reckon they'll be making plans to follow or meet that stagecoach,' Leo told an open-mouthed Jasmine and a blank-faced Charlie. 'We're going to have to move quick to outwit them. I want to pack and set off tonight.'

Jasmine's heavy brows slanted together.

'But how c-could they have found out?'

'We're wasting time,' Leo said impatiently. 'News is out and it don't matter how. Maybe it was Bess here.'

Leo glanced at his dog as he spoke, and Bess wagged her plume of a tail. And just beyond Bess's tail, Leo saw a small brown boot sticking out from under the bed.

'Well, hello! Who might we have a hiding under my bed?'

The boot wriggled and kicked and out from under the bed came a boy of about ten summers. He was covered in dust and his face was tear-streaked, but he bore an unmistakable resemblance to Nathan and Leo had no trouble guessing who he was.

'Another Prescott.'

The boy was bursting with indignation.

'I never thought Matt would tell a secret! We're supposed to be friends and he said if I told him he'd give me a gun, a real gun that had been in the civil war and he never did. But I'd have never told him nothing if I thought he was going to tell.'

Charlie seemed unperturbed that they had a spy in their midst. He sat himself down by the table and fetched out his long brown pipe, but Leo had to jump up and catch Jasmine's arms. She spat like an angry cat.

'Let me go! Jason deserves his ears b-boxing! He hangs around after Matt Brody like a p-puppy. Brother, you're an idiot! Don't you know that Matt runs to Jake with everything?'

Jason hung his head.

'I'll never tell him nothing again.'

'Eavesdropping!' Jasmine said bitterly. 'What would Papa think if he knew that you'd grown up into a boy who sneaks around and listens to private things?' The boy flushed crimson.

'It seemed like fun when Matt did it. We hid under the dining-room table and heard Rose telling Jake he had to sack Hank Miller or she'd never speak to him again.'

Nathan was so surprised that he butted in.

'But Hank's the best stockman Jake has!'

'Yes, but he's married a Mexican and Rose don't like it none because the Mexican lady is called Rosa.'

Leo made up his mind quickly.

'Nathan, will you ride over and see if Hank will help you look after my stock while I'm gone? He and his wife can use the cabin. You'll need help, because I want the scrub bulls weeding out this month.'

'You going to rope the bulls?' Nathan enquired.

'If they was ropable they'd have gone to market with the rest. You can try, if you like. I was thinking of shooting them myself. I want to get in a couple of pure-bred bulls from England. Try to get the quality up—'

Jasmine's small face was indignant.

'Excuse me. If you two gentlemen have quite finished discussing s-stock management I still have a few more things to say to Jason.'

Leo met the boy's repentant brown eyes.

'He knows now, don't you, kid?'

'Yes, sir.'

'And he'll think twice before he follows Matt

62

Brody's example again.'

Jason threw back his shoulders.

'He ain't trusty. I see that now.'

Jasmine looked as if she wanted to say more. Leo knew how to quiet her.

'What did you do with the donkey you stole from Ben at the store?'

Jasmine was torn between laughter and shame and confusion.

'It's in your b-barn. I was going to take it back when nobody was looking.'

'Someone's always looking in this town,' Leo told her.

He peeled off a reasonable number of dollars.

'Nathan, here's money for expenses. And you'd better make up some tale and pay Ben for that donkey, unless you want your sister hanged for horse-stealing.'

Jasmine's face was vivid with eagerness.

'The donkey can carry our stores to C-California. Brilliant.'

Leo gave her a long, long look. She knew what he meant immediately.

'Leo! You can't be so m-mean! I got it all worked out. I'm going to tell Mamma that I'm going to Grandma at Boston. Don't look at me like that. Oh Leo, p-please! I wouldn't slow you down a bit. I'm tough you know. Papa taught me to shoot.'

'Jasmine, you're real smart, I ain't arguing with that. But you're also a sixteen-year-old girl. What're folks going to say if we go off together?'

The thick brows slanted down in a frown.

'B-bother folks! And I'm nearly seventeen.'

'That makes it even worse!'

Jasmine blushed rosily and Leo felt a sudden awkwardness between them. It was relief when Jason piped up eagerly.

'Sir? Sir, would you take me?'

'You're too young as well, and that's final. It's time you two went home.'

Leo expected more argy-bargy, but Jasmine got to her feet docile as a lamb.

'Goodbye and good luck,' she said demurely.

Leo stood at the door and watched the three Prescotts riding off under the starlit night sky before turning back into the warm cabin and looking at Charlie, who was still sitting comfortably by the table. Charlie looked up at Leo and tapped his pipe on the edge of a saucer before carefully laying it aside.

'We leave tonight?' he questioned.

'If you can be ready?'

'I'm ready now. Let's go.'

CHAPTER SIX

Leo was amazed when he found out that the Chinaman knew nothing about horses.

'What do I want with horses in New York?' Charlie protested.

Sighing, Leo walked out into the corral to look over the horses. Nothing but half-broken broncos. He was so fond of his palomino that he rarely rode another beast.

'I guess you'd better take Sunshine. She's the manners of an angel.'

Charlie's reply made Leo realize how little the Chinaman missed.

'No. You think it might be too dangerous to take her. That's why you're riding the black horse.'

He pointed at a horse whose admittedly good conformation was marred by the black and white blotches of a piebald.

'I'll take that one.'

If the piebald had ever been taught anything it seemed to have forgotten it. Leo struggled to get the wild beast tacked up, but Charlie refused to change his mind.

'Can't fall out of this saddle,' he said cheerfully, thrusting his feet into the stirrups. 'If the horse runs away, we'll get there quicker.'

Within hours they had left Leo's land and travelled into the unknown. The first week's journey was uneventful. Charlie kept looking around him, seeing nothing but the bones of twisted rock that rent the landscape and the emptiness of the vast blue sky. At last he delivered his judgement.

'Terrible place! It's all dead.'

But Leo contradicted him.

'You know there's plenty of birds. And see that wavy line in the dust? Snake! A rat-snake or a rattler maybe. See paw-marks over there? Coyote. And if there's coyotes, then there's prey for them to eat. Mice, gophers and the like. It's teeming with life if you know where to look.'

Charlie swatted his hot face.

'Plenty of insects,' he admitted.

A plump bird panicked and flew out of some

low bushes as they approached.

'Look, Charlie! A sage-grouse.'

Leo lifted his rifle - he'd brought his Mississippi as the best all rounder - and took aim. The shot was loud in the hot empty air.

Charlie squinted at the blazing sun. It was lifting towards the top of the sky.

'Time to stop. We'll camp in the shade by those big rocks.'

Charlie was useful around camp. By the time Leo had found the bird he'd shot, then plucked it and drawn it, Charlie had the horses and the donkey hobbled and feeding from their nosebags, the camp equipment tidy and a small fire glowing hot.

'I'm cooking,' said the Chinaman firmly, taking the bird from Leo.

'It's my turn,' Leo protested.

'You're a dreadful cook,' Charlie told him, getting out his precious cooking-pot.

Charlie busied himself with the cooking-pot, adding snips of this and flakes of that from his stores. The fire was almost invisible in the hot sun, but the air above it shimmered with the heat. Leo regarded the Chinaman curiously.

'Did you work in your family restaurant back home?'

Charlie took a long time to answer.

'Sometimes. I guess I was a kind of odd-job boy for the family. I did what I was told. Maybe the West has changed me. I want to be more of a man - like you are.'

'What? I ain't no example for anybody!'

Charlie was about to reply, but a soft sharp sound in the far distance, a rattle or a click of rocks maybe, caught Leo's attention. He took the rifle and quickly shimmied up the side of the rocks under which they were sitting. He scanned in each direction for a good twenty minutes, but nothing moved under the empty sky and nothing disturbed the shimmer of the hot, dry air. Eventually he slid down the rock.

'Dinner's ready,' said Charlie.

Leo took the bowl of stew - boy, that Chinaman could cook! He still felt uneasy.

'We should put out the fire, keep real quiet, if we can.'

Charlie's black eyes twinkled.

'And tomorrow? How do we shoot dinner quietly?'

There was no answering that, but with so far to go they had to eke out their stores when they could. Leo had been thinking about the problem for some time.

'Water's the difficulty. It takes too long to dig enough for the horses. It's months to California by horse. We should have thrown any watchers off the scent by now. Snakebend is about four day's ride, and the stage to San Diego stops there.'

Charlie soon came to a decision.

'I'd be happy to say goodbye to that piebald horse!'

Leo threw Charlie a bedroll and settled himself on his own. They slept away the noon heat, both of them waking as the light went gold and the fierceness went out of the sunshine. He and Charlie mounted their horses and set off, leading the donkey, towards the line of jagged hills. As they travelled, the multicoloured layers of bare rock never seemed to come any closer. That night and the next they walked while the stars came out and the moon rose. When the moon set they slept during the dark hours and rose again before dawn, walking until mid-morning, sleeping away the daytime heat, walking again when it cooled.

Leo fished out his old slingshot and was pleased to find that after a few hours' practice his boyhood skills came back and he was able to knock out a bush-partridge or a rock-rabbit with one clean - quiet - shot. Because it took so long to dig up water, it took them over a week to get to the pass, and Leo was certain they'd made the right decision to take the stagecoach from Snakebend. They drew up their horses at the mouth of the pass.

'You think this path is OK?' asked Charlie. 'It makes my spine crawl.'

'Gives me the creeps, too. If we both feel it, maybe this route ain't so smart.'

Charlie's eyebrows raised in a question.

'What other road can we travel?'

'None,' Leo admitted.

The two men stood looking at the trail that wound though the pass. They were standing in the shadow of the ravine. The air turned icy-cold, as desert air does when the heat goes out of the sun. As the sun sank, the mouth of the pass went dark.

Charlie asked: 'Shall we go in?'

'No. Let's camp now and hit the road at first light. I'd like to be able to see whatever might be waiting for us in that ravine.'

CHAPTER SEVEN

Boulders of all sizes lay scattered over the narrow path that wound through the pass and the horses had to pick their way through loose stone. The sound of their hoofs echoed loudly on the rocky ground. The craggy sides of the ravine caught and magnified every sound. Leo looked up at the narrow strip of blue sky that ran between the cliffs. Large birds circled high above. Their whistling cries echoed and bounced off the rocks in an eerie fashion.

'I wish they'd stay quiet,' Leo muttered. 'I can't hear nothing for them.'

Even the horses seemed to be spooked. His bronco kept shying at nothing and Charlie's piebald kept snorting. When Leo looked back, he saw that the animal's eyes were rolling wildly. They rode on. Nothing happened, but Leo's bad feeling grew worse rather than better, and after an hour he brought his black bronco to a halt.

'This don't feel good, Charlie.'

'You want to go back?'

Leo kept still a minute, but his heart was hammering and all his instincts were yelling at him.

'Yeah.'

The Chinaman kicked at the piebald and tugged at one rein in his clumsy unskilled way. Just as Leo turned his own horse to follow him, the unmistakable hum of a bullet zinging past their noses was rapidly followed by the sound of a gunshot and then its echo. Leo threw down the donkey's rope and left the beast to its own devices.

'Run, Charlie!' he ordered, digging his spurs into the sides of his bronco.

The black horse squealed and reared before springing into a mad gallop. Leo risked a quick glance behind him and was relieved to see Charlie galloping in the right direction after him, although he looked like a sack of potatoes with a flying pigtail. Rope trailing, the donkey was following them both. There was nowhere else for it to go. The high sides of the ravine meant it was impossible to turn off the track.

For a few seconds it seemed that they might succeed in outrunning the gunman. No more shots followed the first, and Leo began to hope they might have gained enough of a head start to run out of the trap.

And then the earth tilted beneath the horses' feet. Leo felt sick and shaken, but he knew - or he thought he knew - what the sensation was because he'd spent some time in San Fransisco when he was younger.

'Earthquake!' he yelled at Charlie.

Charlie had slipped half-out of the saddle and was now clinging onto the horse's black-and-white neck. And just as Leo registered Charlie's plight his ears were assaulted by a rolling rumble of thunder. No, not thunder, there wasn't a cloud in the sky. But the side of the ravine to the left shuddered and then simply dropped away from the skyline. Leo saw dust so thick that it looked like the smoke from an autumn bonfire slowly rise from the side of the hill in rich, rolling clouds. The smoke was followed by tons of earth and rock. The land-slide was moving incredibly quickly. The rocks and boulders travelled first, followed by tons of earth. The landslide rushed towards the centre of the ravine path, directly in front of them, blocking the way.

Leo used all his strength and pulled back on the reins savagely. His bronco was almost too crazed to respond, but eventually it skidded to a halt, sitting down on its haunches like a big dog.

Charlie's piebald was galloping up towards him, the Chinaman only just clinging under its neck. The explosion had sent the beast completely loco. There was no way Charlie could stop it. Leo judged the approach and caught the reins. His arms nearly tore out of their sockets before the horse came to a plunging halt.

The horse stopped so abruptly that Charlie was dislodged completely. He went flying into the air in a perfect parabola, landing about three inches short of the mess of rocks and boulders and newly fallen earth with a loud thud. Leo didn't have time to find the sight amusing. He still held the reins of the piebald horse, and he was suddenly aware that it was behaving oddly.

The horse was juddering all over, its legs folding beneath it, neck arcing, head tilted towards the sky in a frenzy. Leo couldn't think what ailed the beast until the sound and echo of a second gunshot came to his ears and he saw blood spreading in a hot red stain over the white part of the horse's coat. Probably aiming at Leo, their unknown assailant had shot the piebald horse. It fell to the ground next to Charlie who was an unmoving crumpled heap, which suggested he'd hit hard.

Too much was happening but it was vital to take control of the situation. Leo dropped the dead beast's reins and picked up the reins of his own bronco in one hand. His rifle was slung over his saddle-bag and there was no time to get it, so Leo caught up his Colt, dug his heels into the bronco's flanks and yanked the beast around by the mouth, circling, trying to see where the enemy was.

'Over heere, *amigo*!'

The accent. The Spanish word. It told Leo all that he needed to know. Mexican bandits. He circled the horse again, staring, brain processing events like lightning. Understanding the situation was now a matter of life and death. The way out of the pass was blocked. Not by an earthquake but a well-placed stick of dynamite to keep the Mexicans' prey where they wanted it. Leo scanned the sides of the ravine, looking for the bandits.

Small rocks were still falling and fine dust hung in the air like a smoke curtain. There must be one man behind him, the one that had set off the dynamite. There was one man in front of him, the one who had called out. If there were only two of them, then maybe, just maybe, there was a chance.

'Look to your left, *amigo*! I theenk you can see my *compadre*.'

Leo's heart felt raw as he made out the moving outline of a man's hat showing over the top of a boulder. The new bandit was much further away than the twenty-five yard range of his pistol, but Leo didn't put down his gun.

'And to your right, *amigo*. You see?'

Leo saw them all right. Two more bandits. That made five, at least. Even now, he didn't lower his gun. His mouth was dry. It tasted of copper. His mind was working fast, fast, fast. He was aware of the heat of the sun, of the feel of his horse beneath him, the reassuring mass of the gun in his hand. He had to weigh up the situation correctly and make the right move. Anything else would be death.

'We are eight *compadres, amigo*. Better put down your gun.'

Let go of his weapon? In the tightest spot he'd ever been in? It was unthinkable. Was there a way out if he surrendered? Was there any way to get at his rifle without the bandits seeing? Leo's mind raced, but he could think of nothing, except to act beaten and hope for an opening. He let the Colt point, very slightly, towards the ground. The Mexican hurried to encourage him.

'I don't want to keel you. Throw down your gun.'

'You afraid to face me?'

A laugh echoed around the rocks. He couldn't see where the man was hiding.

'Only hell scares me, and I won't go there if I don't keel you. Throw down your gun and you can go home.'

Leo's pistol tilted a little further towards the ground, letting the Mexican believe he was weakening, but he still didn't let go of his weapon. He heard the scrape of hoofs and the Mexican rode out from behind the boulder he'd been hiding behind. Despite the distance that still separated them, too far for either of them to shoot, this gave Leo the chance to size up his adversary. Thin, ragged, desperate, and undisputably dangerous, but maybe not too clever.

Leo's brain moved at furious speed as he assessed the danger he was in. As well as the bandit he could see, he knew for a fact that there were four more guns trained on him, seven more if the Mexican was telling the truth. Yet the urge to defend himself was stronger than the common-sense option of giving in. And was giving in so sensible? To be robbed in this kind of territory would kill a man as surely as a gunshot. Without food or the means to catch it, water or the means to dig for it, he'd be dead in a week.

The Mexican drifted a little closer.

'You're theenking smart, I can see it. Throw down the gun.'

Leo decided. He lowered the gun and the Mexican drifted closer. Thirty-five yards between them now. Close enough. Leo opened his mouth and yelled defiance.

'You want what's mine, you're gonna have to take it.'

He lifted his gun, spurred on his horse to close the gap between him and his target and as soon as he was in range he fired at the bandit. Leo knew that he was insane. There were five guns in total trained on his defenceless body. He got off a second shot, but he then immediately threw himself off his horse and rolled to one side, knowing that he'd be harder to hit while he was in motion.

A bullet hit the stony ground near his head as he scrambled for a boulder where he could take cover. Chips of stone flew in the air, Leo didn't feel a thing, but some of them hit him, because hot blood spurted down his face and ran into his eyes. As soon as he made the cover of the boulder, Leo ripped off the bottom of his shirt-tail and used it to mop his face, especially around his eyes. He needed to see! But before he stuck out his head, he listened hard. He could hear two male voices yelling, but no more gunshots. Then, off in the distance, he heard the donkey bray. That was followed by the loud report of a gun. A scream. Then silence.

Moving slowly, cautiously, Leo poked his head out from behind the boulder. The Mexican he'd been parlaying with was lying on the ground, surrounded by a gory mess of blood and brains. Leo was staggered. He'd aimed at the man's stomach! A glance to the other side showed him that the dead piebald horse still lay on the ground, but Charlie had gone. Leo pulled his head back into the shelter of the rock and tried to work out what he had seen. It didn't add up.

And then he heard the chink of a spurred boot on the rocky ground. Someone was sneaking cautiously towards him. Leo was flooded by an adrenaline rush that took over his whole body. As he lifted his gun he was grinning, joyful, ready for his enemy. Moving as silent as a breath, he backed away, one and then one more pace. He was ready to aim and fire.

As the Mexican came around the edge of the boulder Leo seemed to have all the time in the world to examine him. The Mexican's face contracted into a snarl as he spotted Leo, but the man's thin claw seemed to lift his gun so slowly that Leo had sized up the situation and fired his own trusty Navy Colt before the bandit was anywhere near ready to act. Because the Mexican's gun was pointed so low, there was no need to attempt the difficult task of taking the man's gun out of his hand. Instead, Leo fired at the man's soft belly, aiming for the navel, knowing that the shot would drop the bandit in his tracks. And it did.

The impact threw the man's body back and jerked his head forward, folding him in the middle. He threw his arms wide, dropping the gun to the rocky ground. Leo tensed in case the dropped gun fired, but nothing happened and he relaxed again, turning back to the Mexican to see if it would take another shot to finish the man.

Leo had been lucky. The bullet must have torn a major blood-vessel in the bandit's groin. Blood rose in the air like a fountain then fell to soak the ground around the body. Leo stood ready to fire again, but the bandit never moved and all Leo had to do was watch until the gush of blood spluttered to a stop and the man was no longer breathing. Leo was thankful that he wouldn't have to administer a *coup de grâce* in cold blood. But his blood had no business going cold. He'd seen only two dead Mexicans, and he knew there were five of them - at least. He turned, meaning to see what was happening in the ravine, but as he took the first step, a girl's voice called.

'Leo! Leo, w-where are you?'

He was dead and he was dreaming. The Mexican had killed him, not the other way around. How else could he explain hearing Jasmine Prescott's voice in the middle of a Mexican ambush in the middle of the desert a good three weeks' ride from her ranch? Yet heat of the sun felt real enough and the smell of blood was real enough to have the big birds he'd noticed earlier circling so low that he could identify them as vultures with bare necks, yellow talons and hooked, rapacious beaks.

'Leo?' the voice called again.

And this time he had to accept it was real.

'Jasmine?'

He was answered by a joyful squeal. A flying figure rounded the boulder and sprang at him. She flung her arms around his neck and kissed him. Leo could see she looked different somehow, but the slanting black eyebrows were the same and so were the merry dark eyes full of energy and mischief. Then Leo saw what she'd changed.

'Your Mom's gonna hit the moon when she sees your hair! What in thunder made you cut it off?'

Jasmine simply laughed.

'I'm disguised as a b-boy, silly! I'm coming to the g-goldfields with you.'

Her neat little figure was clad in men's jeans and she was wearing a leather waistcoat over an old check shirt. Leo took another look at the sweet curves under the waistcoat and the peach of her bottom and he couldn't help yelling.

'You're crazier than a moonbug if you think you look anything like a boy!'

He saw a shadow touch her eyes.

'If I c-cut my hair shorter?'

'Jasmine - it ain't about hair! Even if you was bald, you couldn't hide your shape or the way that you walk. You can't go to no goldfields and that's final.'

The black brows slanted down and she gave an angry jerk of her chin.

'You men wouldn't be going anywhere if I hadn't been here to s-shoot the Mexicans!'

'Leo! Where did you get to?' shouted a cheerful voice.

Charlie hobbled as he came around the boulder, and there was blood on his blue suit, but he was grinning and he was in one piece. And then Leo heard the patter of feet and round the boulder after Charlie came the small figure of a boy.

'Leo! Hi! You never saw us a bit, did you? It was really keen following you both and you never knowing. And just think. I've been in my first gun-battle. I'm only ten, so I think that's pretty good, don't you? I killed the most important one. Jasmine told me to sneak up on the bandit who did the dynamiting so he couldn't shoot us from behind. I shot him from the side and he didn't see me, but he was carrying a gun, so that's sporting, ain't it? Oh, wow! You killed one as well. Charlie got two.'

Leo looked at Charlie and raised his eyebrows. The Chinaman shrugged and spread out his hands as if he'd no idea how Mexicans got dead, but Jason had no such inhibitions.

'You should have seen Charlie! It was awesome. He kind of made an axe out of his hands and chopped at the bandits, and blam! They fell over dead. Will you teach me how to do that, Charlie? Will you, please? I'd sure like to whack that Matt Brody a few chops.'

Charlie shrugged.

'I should be dead. I don't know why they didn't shoot me.'

The answer became clear as they checked the bodies. All five of the bandits - the extra three must have been an invention - were skeleton-thin. They had no food. They had no water. And the few rounds they'd fired must have been their last.

'Look at these weapons!' mused Leo. 'They're the old five-shot Colts. You can't even get the ammunition for them nowadays.'

'No water! Leo, how did they think they were going to live in the desert?'

'Maybe they had to leave in a hurry. Well, It don't matter now. Charlie, you lost your piebald friend, so you'd better choose the best of the Mexicans' horses.'

Leo turned and was about to walk over to catch his own bronco, but Jasmine rushed up to him and pulled at his sleeve. Her skin was chalk-white and the pupils of her eyes were wide and staring.

'You're not g-g-g-going to l-l-leave them u-un-b-b-b-buried?'

For all her bravery, she was just a little girl. Leo met her anguished eyes.

'First time you shot a man?'

He saw the white skin of her throat move as she swallowed.

'I'll never threaten to b-blow anyone's brains out again. B-brains are m-messy.'

He admired her courage.

'I'll bury your Mexicans for you, if you want it.'

'Please. I don't want those h-horrible birds p-pecking at them. They were men, after all.'

'They was outlaws and robbers as well and the world's a better place without them,' Leo told her. 'But I'll see to them for you.'

Easier said than done. There was no digging a grave in the hard rock of the ravine. They didn't have enough fuel to make a funeral pyre. There was nothing but rock, and it was going to take a lot of rocks to cover the bodies. Leo thought of the labour it would entail and was wishing Jasmine at Jericho until Charlie came up with a plan.

'There's a deep cleft in the ravine over here,'

he announced. 'How about putting in the bodies, then putting rocks on top? Make a good grave, I think.'

Even so, it was dark before they finished. By common consent they moved on along the ravine, away from the killing-ground. Nobody wanted to camp within sight or smell of the blood-soaked ground, let alone listen to vultures ripping at the dead horse. When the moon came up they could move a little faster. Leo breathed easier with each mile they travelled away from the ambush. A few hours later they came to a pebbled beach that lay alongside a dry water-course that crossed the ravine.

Leo swung himself off his bronco.

'Jason, you start digging water for the horses. Charlie, can you light a fire and start cooking? I'll make camp.'

A small, indignant voice by his elbow spoke sharply.

'Do you have any embroidery for m-me to do?'

'Gimme a break, Jasmine!'

But Leo had to admit she was neat and handy to have around camp, unlike her little brother who was willing but clumsy. Charlie's Mexican horse never seemed to have encountered a nose-bucket before. Jason spilt a lot of water before

Jasmine gave her rich chuckle and took over. Leo was glad to hear her laugh. She'd been far too white and quiet while they'd been burying the Mexicans.

Charlie made them biscuits dripping with hot jam, and they drank sweet tea with whiskey in it before lying down to sleep. Leo fell asleep at once, but he woke up in the cold of the early dawn, feeling as if someone had called him. He got up swiftly and checked the camp. All was in order, but sitting on the little beach, away from the others, was Jasmine. When Leo went over he found that her face was wet.

'Oh, Leo, I'm thinking about the man that I s-shot. He must have had a m-mother, or sisters maybe, waiting for him. . . .'

Leo put his arm around her and let her cry for a while. He'd never held a weeping girl before, but he soothed her as though she was a puppy or a horse and it seemed to do the trick. He sat feeling her soft body and breathing in her sweet smell, and found that he liked the sensation. He didn't know whether Jasmine would feel better or worse if she knew that the bandit she'd shot in the head had also taken two of Leo's bullets in his belly, so he didn't tell her. He didn't know what to say, so he sat quiet. Eventually Jasmine sniffed and dried her eyes on the sleeve of her check shirt.

'He was going to k-kill you, Leo, and I'm not sorry that I shot him, but I needed to feel s-sad a bit before it all came right in my mind.'

She sat upright and Leo took away his arm from her shoulders. He looked down at her. Her face was a white heart in the dimness.

'I won't be soft any more. I'll need to be t-tough in the goldfields.'

'I can't take you.'

'Why? Why not? Haven't I p-proved how useful I can be?'

'The goldfields are dangerous. There ain't no law out there, you know, 'cept what people decide is the law and administer right there and then.'

'I'm n-not afraid.'

The first dawn light was lightening the colour of the sky. Leo looked down at the unmistakable femininity of the slight form sitting next to him. Her newly cut hair was already curling into pretty dark ringlets.

'I'm afraid for you,' he replied soberly.

Jasmine examined his face, searching his eyes for the truth.

'It's never any use a-arguing with you,' she said sadly.

'Snakebend's a couple of days' ride from here. I'm gonna send you home on the stagecoach.'

A sigh ran through her body and she looked up and met his eyes ruefully.

'It's a waste of good hair. Are you sure the gold-miners won't think I'm a b-boy?'

'Not for a minute.'

Leo heard Charlie getting up behind them. The Chinaman rattled his cooking pots and that woke Jason, who started chattering even before his eyes opened. It was time to get moving. Leo took Jasmine's little chin in his hand and tilted it up towards him, so that he could look into her eyes, anxious to make her understand.

'I won't take you to a place where I can't protect you. I want your word that you'll go home and take your little brother with you.'

She gave him a long, sad look, but at last she gave in.

'I p-promise.'

CHAPTER EIGHT

Leo and Charlie stood in the middle of the dirty track that was Snakebend's main street and watched the back of the stagecoach bounce and rattle on its way to Hope Town.

'Think we'll find her waiting in San Diego?' Charlie asked.

Leo shook his head.

'She'd never break her word.'

'Our stagecoach leaves in an hour. How many days to San Diego?'

'I don't want to think about it! Man, I hate the way those coaches bounce.'

'I agree. Worse way to travel than piebald horse.'

'Charlie! I'll make a horseman of you yet! You want to throw away that ticket and buy a new horse?'

'Wouldn't mind! But I guess we got to get a move on.'

'I guess so,' Leo agreed. 'Stagecoach is quickest.'

But by the time they staggered off the stagecoach in San Diego he felt as if he'd rather have his toenails pulled out than go anywhere in a stagecoach ever again. And they were still three days' travel from the goldfields. Charlie said he'd buy the new tickets.

'I'll get them, Charlie. You stand out too much.'

'You think people are still looking for us?'

'They wouldn't be looking for me and a Mexican. How about I cut off your pigtail and buy you some Mexican gear?'

Charlie clutched his pigtail. Teasing Charlie cheered up Leo slightly, but the next leg of the journey turned out to be the worst. The road was so cut up it was nothing but ruts. The places they stopped served the worst food on the planet. And as for the so-called hotel they were told to sleep in. . . .

Just after dusk on the third day they rolled, rattled and bounced into the shanty town that had sprung up around the goldfields. Thanks to the money from Charlie's nuggets they could afford to stay in the best hotel. Two tin baths were set side by side by the fire and then filled up to the brim with pitchers of hot water.

'This is the life,' Leo mused. 'Cold water does me at home, but this is grand.'

Charlie worked up a fine lather and then sponged his face with it.

'I know what I'll do when I go home. I'll buy a railway and make lots of money.'

'Aren't there enough railways already?'

'Stagecoach and train going to the same place. Which one you take?'

Leo's bones were still aching from the trip.

'No contest! You'll make a fortune.'

They turned into wonderfully comfortable twin beds with white sheets. Leo slept dreamlessly and he woke early feeling refreshed. Charlie was up and making plans. He turned over his precious map to show Leo a list of tools and equipment written on the other side. Charlie turned his back, fumbled under his blue suit, and then handed Leo a roll of money and the list.

'Somebody maybe looking for us. Best you go alone.'

The prices the storekeepers were charging were more than Leo could stomach at first but, after asking around all morning, he realized that he couldn't buy cheaper.

'Used to be way more expensive,' said the man who sold him a mule. 'Two years ago I would have gotten five times what you paid me for a fine beast like this.'

Leo looked at his meagre amount of change.

'I'm starving. Any suggestions?'

'Try Ma Bateman's pie-shop. You might survive one of her meat-and-potato pies, but then again, you might not.'

'Thanks. I'll risk it.'

Leo bought his pie and took it out onto the street to eat so that he could keep an eye on his mule. The street thronged with Americans from all over the country, and a sprinkling of Indians, Mexicans, Chinamen, and Blacks walked past him, ninety-nine per cent of them male. All of the faces were strange to him. Except one: a tall, thin man with a face exactly like his own. The man was wearing an ordinary suit rather than a frock-coat, but he carried a Bible and wore a white neckcloth. Leo's heart gave a twist and he looked again, but there was no mistake. Walking towards him was his elder brother, Theodore.

Not knowing how to react, Leo drew back against the wall of the pie-shop and watched his brother pass. Theo glanced at him and walked by. It was ten years since the brothers had spoken, and Leo had kept the beard he'd grown on the journey, but still, he was surprised his brother hadn't recognized him. He'd known Theo at once.

Leo felt thoughtful as he walked back to the hotel. It seemed to him that his brother's face had changed. Theo had been the kind of Holy Roller who spent all his time worrying about Hell and shouting about the sins that might send a man there. But if Theo had mellowed, then Leo would like to know about it.

Leo was too deep in his thoughts to pay attention to what was going on about him. He simply led the mule straight into the stable round the back of the hotel. It took a bellow in a voice he knew from Hope Town to alert him to his surroundings.

'Stan? Where you got to, Stanley?'

Leo thought he must be losing his grip! He had to be imagining Jake Brody's voice, but he listened keenly for the reply.

'I'm right here, Jake. Why are you yelling at me?'

'Because I'm paying you to stand watch, you moron! A platoon of Leo Denvers could have waltzed past you!'

'I was taking a leak, that's all, Jake, but I never turned me back. I was still watching. He ain't back yet.'

Cold sweat ran down Leo's back and he drew into the shadow of the stable. It was Jake Brody, all right. No mistaking those cold, near-set blue eyes, the bull-like neck and the tight curls of his blond hair. Leo didn't know Stan. He was a thin man and his front teeth stuck out like a rat's.

'You got the Chinkie, Jake?'

'Yeah, he's back at camp. But he ain't got the map. Damn Leo Denver's sneaked away with it. And I want it. And I'm going to possess it. And if I find out you was derelict in your duty in any way. . . .'

Stan looked alarmed. He wasn't so much a stranger, then. He obviously knew how dangerous Jake Brody could be.

'I was looking all the time I was peeing. I promise you.'

'Nobody obstructs me for long. I reckon I'll rupture that Chinaman's bones one by one until he decides to draw me a new map.'

Jake strode off and as he vanished through the back door of the hotel Stan visibly relaxed. Leo stayed tense. If Jake was lying in wait then Leo couldn't go back to the hotel room. He didn't know a soul in California and Charlie had the money, so how could Leo rescue the Chinaman? Jake's threats of torture were not idle. He had a mean streak in him that came out in his treatment of animals or the men who worked for him. Leo had to get moving. He checked around the stable but there was no way out other than the way he'd walked in, so he set himself to watching Stanley.

Stan wasn't much of a watchman. He had a bottle stashed inside a bucket close to him and he was mostly interested in refreshing himself with large swigs of whiskey. Leo stood like a statue in the shadow of the stable. All he had to do was wait for the inevitable moment when Nature would call again.

Thirty minutes later Stan turned his back to relieve himself. Leo sprang out of the stable and through the entrance of the stable yard and shot into the street all in one rapid movement. Stan didn't see him go any more than he'd noticed him arrive.

Once in the open street Leo was assailed by dizziness. He had nowhere to go and he knew that he was hunted. He needed some money. And he needed to find out where Charlie was and he needed to beat the living daylights out of Jake Brody and he didn't know how to make a start on any of it.

'Whoa!' he told himself. 'What's your first step here?'

The answer was clear. There was only one person he had a claim on in this town. He would have to find his brother and somehow persuade Theo to help him rescue Charlie.

CHAPTER EIGHT

Theo took some tracking down. Most men on the street were too drunk to tell you where their mothers lived, let alone a preacher, and Leo had no more luck asking in the crowded, verminous bars. The last one was vile. Reeling from the smell of smoke, vomit and rough whisky, Leo left fast, wanting fresh air. As he lifted the tattered sack that covered the entrance hole he collided with a sturdy figure who was walking in. To his surprise Leo saw that he'd bumped into a woman. An older woman, with a line of dark hair on her upper lip. She was wearing clothes that looked as if they were made from sacks, but the white apron she wore over her skirt was clean and so was her face.

'Ma'am, I surely wouldn't recommend this place to you.'

She looked at him and Leo saw that she had the most beautifully-shaped blue eyes. They shone with a loving expression that put him in mind of his mother. He couldn't help smiling back at her. She showed him a Bible.

'It's kind of you to think of my welfare, stranger. But I'm afraid of nothing while I trust in Jesus.'

Leo grabbed her arm so urgently that she looked surprised.

'Do you know other churchgoers, ma'am? Do you know Theo Denver?'

A wide smile.

'I'm Mrs Denver, Theo's wife.'

'I'm looking for him real urgent.'

'I'll take you to him. We don't live far away.'

Leo decided that Mrs Denver was an angel because she asked him no awkward questions as he followed her through a rundown area of home-made shacks. The smell made it clear there was no plumbing in any of the habitations. The older woman stopped by a strangely shaped wooden structure. Theo's shack was made from sawn-up barrels. Inside however, it was cosy. A fire burned in a stone fireplace and a home-made tin-can chimney-stack took away all the smoke. Theo sat on an empty dynamite box by the fire, reading a big black book. He looked up and saw his wife. He dropped the prayer book he'd been holding and jumped to his feet. His expression was agonized.

'Jessie! You were going to read the Bible to those sinners in the bar. What stopped you?'

'All is well, Mr Denver.'

At this reassurance the expression on Theo's face broke into such relief and happiness that Leo guessed his brother had much been changed by marriage. Mrs Denver pattered across the room and bent tenderly over a rough wooden box next to the fire. Leo got a shock when Theo joined his wife in looking into the orange-box. Their doting expressions gave Leo a clue, but he was still surprised to see a bundle wrapped in sacking with ten pink toes poking out of the bottom of the sack. A baby! His own brother with a baby! Leo stood still, getting over the idea that he was an uncle while Mrs Denver cooed over her baby. Then she turned and smiled at Leo.

'Mr Denver, my dear. I'm forgetting my manners. We have a visitor.'

Theo moved towards Leo with a warm smile and an automatic greeting.

'Welcome, brother, welcome.'

He put out his hand, then his fingers froze in mid-air and his jaw dropped open.

'Leo? Little Leo? Is it really you?'

Leo was enveloped in a massive hug. He put his arms around his older brother and hugged him in return. When Theo slapped Leo's back one last time and let go, tears gleamed in the older man's eyes.

'How long have you been in town?'

'You walked past me today.'

Theo snapped his fingers.

'So that's why I've been thinking about you all afternoon.'

Mrs Denver smiled and rearranged her shawl so that it protected her baby. 'Praise the Lord! You two men will have much to talk over. I'll take the baby to visit poor Brett Walton, Mr Denver, dear.'

'Don't stay too long.'

Leo watched the light in Jessie Denver's loving eyes as she said goodbye and thought he'd never seen a finer woman.

'Theo, I'm real happy to find you settled.'

'And I am happy to find you, little brother. But I prayed that we'd be reunited. The Lord brought you here.'

'Maybe he did,' Leo answered. 'Theo, I need

help. You'll understand when I tell you my story.'

But Leo hit an absolute rock wall. Theodore was adamant.

'Leo, it pains me to say no to you after all that's passed between us. I was a miserable sinner in the old days, for all that I thought I was doing the business of the Lord. I've changed a lot, Leo, since I met Jessie. But I could never aid you in a venture that will end in killing, and from what you tell me it will, won't it?'

Leo couldn't deny it.

'I can't abandon Charlie.'

'The Lord moves in mysterious ways. It may be a part of his plan.'

Leo felt uncomfortable, but he had to tell the truth as he saw it.

'It seems to me that leaving Charlie in the hands of Jake Brody would be a worse sin than killing a man to prevent it.'

Theo jumped to his feet and paced. The fire-light glowed red on his face.

'Let me read the Bible to you and maybe the Lord's words will persuade you.'

'Theo, I'm real glad we're friends again. But I have to go find Charlie now.'

Leo moved towards the door of the shack. His brother followed him. 'What can you do on your own? Stay here, Leo! I won't let you go.'

Leo shook his head stubbornly.

'At least let us pray together before you go.'

'There's no time. Jake Brody could be torturing Charlie while we speak.'

Theodore pushed ahead of Leo and blocked the way out of the shack. He held up his hand. His eyes shone with some of the old fanaticism.

'One prayer together.'

While Leo was trying to think how to say 'no' without getting into an argument, he heard a gunshot and another. The sack that did duty as a door spun out and he saw Theo jerk and shudder. His brother's face looked utterly surprised. Then it contorted in pain. Then his whole body collapsed forward into the shack. Leo reached up and caught his brother's body. He lowered it to the beaten-earth floor of the shack. Leo's heart was thumping so fast he felt sick.

'Theo? How bad are you?'

Leo grabbed his brother's head and turned it so that he could see his face. There was blood. There was too much blood around. Theo looked up at him. His eyes were blazing with joy and his face was bright.

'At last! I'll meet my Saviour.'

'Theo! You ain't that bad. You can't leave your

baby. You can't leave Jessie.'

But Theo's body jerked and grew heavy in Leo's arms. Leo held his brother's body tightly and couldn't believe what was happening. He heard a murmur, and quickly bent his head to listen to the soft words. He could have sworn that his brother was happy. Theo's tone was exultant.

'Light! Tell Jessie! The light is so beautiful.'

And Theo was gone.

Leo knelt on the earth floor holding the body, unwilling to let go. Unwilling to believe in this sudden disaster. How could this be? How could he have found Theo again only to have him snatched away by cruel chance? His brother's body seemed to cool rapidly. Leo let him go and got to his feet. He looked down at Theo for instant longer, stricken by his loss. He never forgot that moment. But he had work to do, and he had to collect his mind. His brother had been shot twice in the back and there was a great deal of blood. He needed to cover the body. He'd better get two blankets at least.

Leo turned for the bed, which was wooden and curtained with sacks. Then he froze as he heard boots approaching the door. Cautious, furtive boots. Leo drew his gun, then he hesitated a second and slipped behind the home-made headboard. He kept the gun steady on the shadow in the doorway, but he didn't shoot. Leo wanted to know what was happening around here. He drew further back into the shadows and listened hard. A voice he'd never heard before called out.

'Hey, Jake! This is really good! I killed him all right.'

As Leo registered the meaning of these words, a feeling worse than pain seized his heart. Unwittingly, he'd killed his brother. He hadn't know it, he hadn't meant to, but he'd drawn the gunmen and caused the death. Bitter, bitter regrets filled his mind. It took all his self-control to stand still as a man walked into the room and stood over the body. Leo lifted his gun and took careful aim. The firelight lit the face of a man with the blond hair and blue eyes of Scandinavian origins. Leo didn't know him. This man was a hired gun in the pay of Jake Brody, and Leo knew on whom he sought revenge. He knew who was to blame for this, and he swore as he stood in the shadows that he'd kill Jake Brody. But the second set of boots stopped outside the hut and didn't come in. While Leo was weighing up the situation he heard what

Jake was calling through the door and realized that he'd better hold his trigger-finger still.

'Well, get the map and get of there, Gus. I want to get back to that Chinkie!'

It was hard watching a stranger pawing his brother's body.

'There's no map.'

'Look again, you jerk.'

'Look yourself. There ain't no map.'

Jake poked his bull-like head in through the doorway. Leo wondered whether Jake would realize that he was looking at the wrong brother, but blood had soaked Theo's collar so that he no longer looked like a preacher and Jake searched the corpse without noticing a thing.

'That Chinkie was telling me lies! Denver ain't got no map.'

The hired gun looked down at Theo. His expression was puzzled.

'Denver looked bigger from the hotel window.'

'He always was a runt and now he's dead. Come on!'

Jake backed out of the shack doorway. It took all Leo's will to watch that stocky figure go out of range. His heart wanted to shoot him so bad he could taste it. But there was Charlie to consider, and Jake would be off his guard, believing that Leo was dead. He'd be easy to follow. Maybe Leo could rescue Charlie, and then. . . .

Jake Brody, you'll get what you deserve for killing my brother!

His brother's death hit him all over again with a hammer blow. But Leo couldn't sit still and grieve. Not for him the luxury of mourning. He had to decide what to do next. It was a hard decision, but if he waited for Mrs Denver to return he'd lose his chance to find out where Charlie was being held captive.

It was a dreadful business, covering his brother's lifeless, blood-soaked body with the blankets from the bed. The blankets were made from stitched-together sacks. Leo felt steel claws gripping his throat so that he could hardly breathe, but there was no time to stay and mourn over his poor brother's body. Jake was already gone and he had to follow him – now – or lose the chance for ever.

Leo pushed aside the bullet-torn sack and made his way through the stinking huddle of shacks. Nobody looked out to see who was walking by or what the shooting had been about. Full night had fallen outside and it took Leo's eyes a few minutes to adjust. Jake Brody couldn't be that far away. Leo had spent only a few seconds, a minute at most, covering his brother's corpse.

Looking left and right Leo soon saw his quarry, moving fast in the dark night, and moving openly as well. Jake Brody had no idea he was in danger. Leo felt satisfaction fill his heart and numb some of the pain he was feeling. He followed as silently as a moth, keeping well back in the shadows. The two men went around the back of a cheap hotel and entered the stable. They burrowed into a pile of straw and went to sleep. Leo found a spot in the yard where he could sit and watch the door. He dozed, but very lightly, and woke at dawn when the men stirred. Jake Brody handed Gus a fat roll of money.

'Half for the shooting and half for stores. You load up and fetch them out after me. I want to get back to camp and check on those hired guns.'

Gus took the money and went back into the stable. Jake tacked up his horse and galloped down the street. Leo slipped after him, but Brody whipped up his horse and there was no way a man on foot could follow. Leo watched his enemy out of sight, noted that Brody was travelling east and went back to the stable. Gus was a snoring heap. Leo took out his Colt. The sound of the Navy's trigger cocking brought Gus awake in an instant. Leo wasn't giving him a chance to escape.

'Where's Brody's camp?'

He could see a lie forming in the blue eyes before the killer spoke.

'Westerly. He's on claim sixty-five.'

Leo saw triumph in the man's face. He thought Leo was stupid enough to swallow his lies. Anger overwhelmed Leo's common sense. He pulled the trigger. A dull click was the only response. Gus took immediate advantage. He reached for his own gun. Leo remembered Theo's blood gushing and wondered whether it had touched his ammunition. He couldn't trust his gun. If it failed again Gus would shoot him. Leo threw the gun aside and reached for a shovel that was leaning on the stable wall. In another fraction of a second Gus would be ready to fire. There was no time to think, plan or aim. The barrel of his enemy's gun seemed to sprout two wide, black, menacing mouths, but Leo ran towards the lethal weapon, lifting the shovel over his head and bringing it down towards Gus's shoulder on the side of the arm that was control-ling the gun.

The shovel hit the blond man's shoulder at

exactly the same time as he squeezed the trigger. The impact twisted the man's body to one side and spoiled his aim. The gun fired, but the bullet missed Leo and passed through the wooden wall of the stable. The noise set the horses whinnying and stamping, but nobody came to see to them.

Leo lifted the shovel once more and smashed it down on Gus's gun hand. The shovel hit so hard that the impact shattered the handle, which splintered and broke. But it had done its job. The gun spun out of Gus's hand and skittered across the beaten-earth floor, disappearing into the pile of straw that he had been sleeping in.

Although Gus's right arm was hanging and useless, he was a bold fighter. He sprang for a rake that leaned on the wall behind him and the farm implement whistled through the air as it headed for Leo. He twisted away and lifted his right arm to protect his head. The rake caught his ear a massive blow and landed so hard on his shoulder that Leo heard a bone crack. His right arm didn't want to move, so Leo reached out clumsily with his left hand and grabbed for a pitchfork that had been leaning next to the rake. The prongs of the pitchfork made a better

110

weapon than the tines of a rake, but the shaft was smaller and Gus had the better reach.

The Scandinavian was already moving in for the next blow. He aimed low, swiping at Leo's ankles, trying to knock him over with a massive strike. Leo staggered, but his boots protected him from the worst of the blow, and the rake-head smashed into the ground. The handle of the rake shattered, leaving the killer weaponless. Leo took immediate advantage. Using his left hand, he lifted the pitchfork. Leo saw fear changing the shape of Gus's face.

'Don't hit me! I'll tell you!' the man squealed.

Leo drew back the pitchfork.

'Don't kill me! Easterly. Brody's camping on N37 on the East Road.' The pitchfork was poised. Leo looked right into the man's eyes.

'You killed my brother.'

And he rammed the pitchfork home, aiming the double curved prongs at the ribs over the killer's heart. Gus stumbled backwards and banged up against the wall of the stable as the pitchfork hit. One prong ran in true. Pink blood foamed out, bubbling with air from the lungs. The other prong skidded on bone. Leo twisted the shaft of the pitchfork and pushed again. This time the prong sank into Gus's body and smashed through the rib to pierce the soft heart. Leo could feel the weight of the man on the end of the fork. Gus couldn't speak – bubbles of froth foamed at his lips – but his eyes met those of Leo's, and there was understanding in them and an acceptance of his punishment. Leo held the pitchfork fast.

'You killed my brother,' he repeated.

And he held the pitchfork steady until the man died.

Leo limped as he left the stable and his right shoulder wouldn't move. There was no time for doctoring. He was burning to go after Brody, but it was his duty to check on his sister-in-law, so he headed for Theo's shack. Leo pushed back the sack and then came to a full halt in the doorway.

The shack was full of people, clustering around an open mahogany coffin that lay on some home-made trestles in the middle of the room. Leo would have backed away, but Jessie Denver looked up and saw him. Her lovely eyes were sober, but Leo saw concern for him in her expression.

'Leo, I've been praying for you and your sin all night.'

The hostile expressions of the other people in the room reminded Leo that his face was bruised and his clothes were stiff and marked with dried blood. Everyone thought he'd killed his brother and run away. Their eyes called him a murderer, and they were afraid. They shuffled their feet and backed away from him.

'Oh, ma'am, excuse me, but you are so wrong! I've been away after the man that shot my brother.'

Leo did a rapid count of the men in the room. Thirteen. More than enough to take out Jake Brody. He looked at each whiskered face in turn.

'I know where the killer is if any of you men would care to follow me and make the scumbag pay for shooting Theo!'

'It's our Christian duty to turn the other cheek!' Jessie cried. 'I forbid it.'

Leo saw that none of the men in the room had any intention of forming a shooting-party with or without Jessie's permission. Pacifists one and all. Jessie brought Leo a tin pail full of water. The smell and taste of it was ambrosia.

'Slowly,' she warned him. 'Your stomach will cramp if you drink too much at once. Now, let me see to that shoulder.'

She said the bone was broken and swiftly bound it up. Leo wondered again at the character of this woman. Her husband was lying dead behind her and she had room in her heart for his brother's welfare.

'Is your arm strong enough to be one of the pall-bearers? It's your right as his kin, and it'll comfort you to pay him this last service.'

The sound of hurried boots at the door announced the presence of a latecomer.

'Mrs Denver. I heard the terrible news. Theo was a fine man, and he'll be a great loss to us all.'

'Mr O'Connor, I do thank you. Come in. My husband would have been proud to have you carry his coffin.'

'John O'Connor!' ejaculated Leo.

The bounty hunter's green eyes opened wide in surprise, but this was no time for talking. The other pall-bearers stepped forward, the coffin lid was hammered down, and Leo found himself carrying his brother's corpse over the muck of the shanty area and down the main street of the town.

Although the shooting had taken place only hours before, word was out. Leo was humbled at the huge number of people who joined in the crowd walking behind his brother's coffin. Jessie marched at the head of them all, and her voice rose high in a hymn. Other voices joined hers. By the time they reached a scruffy patch of ground on the outskirts of town more than a hundred people were singing.

The town's cemetery was marked by a lopsided fence and few of the graves were marked, but Jessie seemed not to notice her surroundings. She concentrated fiercely on the words of the preacher who was holding the service. The prayers seemed to bring her comfort. Leo realized that he must tell her about her husband's last words. After the burial, Leo pushed his way through the crowd of mourners and took her to one side. Her fine eyes glowed as she heard how Theo had died.

'Thank you,' she said. 'Those words are precious.'

Another man pressed forward, wanting to talk to her, and another, and she was swept away. Leo suddenly wondered who was looking after the baby and who would look after Jessie now. As Theo's brother, it was his duty to make sure they were cared for, yet he had Charlie to worry about as well. Leo put a hand to his forehead as he tried to reconcile his responsibilities. John O'Connor came forward and spoke to him.

'Why stand out in the sun when there's shade to be had round the side of this buggy?'

Leo was glad to see a familiar face in the

middle of a town full of strangers, and gladder still to think he might have found an ally. He poured out his story to the bounty hunter. John looked at him with his green, catlike eyes.

'I've three hundred dollars – less the price of my horse and the clothes I stand up in – but I'll do what I can.'

Leo remembered the $4,000 bounty.

'You're broke already?

'If I tell you that I met up with some gold miners, and that there was a pony race involved and a good game of cards and maybe a few girls and a glass of whiskey thrown in, I think you'll get the gist of it.'

'I'm surprised you've three hundred dollars left.'

O'Connor's mouth split in a self-deprecating grin.

'I had nothing left, but I brought in Fred Hindle yesterday. Three hundred is a small bounty, but then, he wasn't so hard to catch. I came looking for Mrs Denver to pay her my debts. She's a fine woman, your sister-in-law. She fed me and clothed me and, to tell you the truth, she pointed out what a fool I was. I had nothing left in the world other than my lucky Cherokee pistol.'

'Maybe you was cheated?'

'No, no, those miners are as good a bunch of boys as you could hope to meet. How about we go find them? They'll go after Jake Brody. I'll get them started with what's left of my bounty, and you can reward them properly when we get the gold.'

'Do you know where they are? We need to move fast!'

John O'Connor found the men easily enough. There were seven of them sleeping in a reeking shanty. They'd drunk all their money and they weren't too hard to talk into a paying adventure before they went back to their gold-claims.

'Tell the truth, I'm thinking of giving up gold-panning,' one said. 'You can make more in Chicago on them road-gangs they got going.'

'You'll never get rich working for someone else,' argued another.

'At least I'd get what I got regular. And a man's got a right to socialize. There's women in Chicago.'

'Get going! You can talk while we're moving,' ordered Leo.

It took an inordinate amount of argy-barging and planning to get seven hungover men and one bounty hunter on the road. The second Leo thought he had it all together, John O'Connor insisted that he had to visit with Jessie before leaving.

'Don't let her talk you out of the rescue!' Leo warned grimly. Then he softened. 'And tell her not to leave town until I get back. She's my kin now, and I aim to look after her.'

Leo and the other men set off via the hotel where Leo had left his mule. He'd borrowed a horse, but he needed the mule and the stores. He couldn't show himself, or Jake Brody might get word that his adversary wasn't dead, so Leo had to talk one of the men into acting for him. Nobody wanted to do it. The others pushed forward a man called Brett.

'I don't want to go. What if they take me for a thief?'

Leo gazed into Brett's scared, obstinate eyes. It would be so much easier if Leo could fetch the mule himself, but he couldn't risk it.

'I'll write you a chit to say that I sold you the mule and stores. And once we've rescued Charlie, you can keep the beast.'

Greed kicked in and Brett took the chit. His friends watched him walk towards the hotel. One of them said to Leo:

'Brett's brother was hanged because of a mix-up about who owned a horse!'

The other men had their own opinions.

'Mix-up, my left foot! His brother was guilty as Cain.'

'He never took that horse.'

'Excuse me, gentlemen. Can we discuss this as we ride?'

'Sure, Leo. Hey, how you getting on with that nag of mine? You want to buy it when we're done?'

'I'll see,' Leo replied diplomatically.

His borrowed mount was a slug with an iron mouth, but he wasn't going to say anything that might cause the men to stop and argue. They rode out of town and took the trail towards the claim where Brody was camping. Anxiety driving him on, Leo refused to stop until they were about a mile past the marker for N37. It would have been safer to have kept going another mile, but he could see that mutiny was brewing.

'Take a break, fellas!'

'About time!' they grumbled.

The men were messy campers. They tethered their horses so carelessly that Leo was tempted to do it over again in case the beasts escaped. They dropped gear where it was certain to be trodden on. They lit a wastefully large fire. Leo bit his tongue. They were a temporary crew and their manners were none of his business.

The sound of horses in the distance set his heart to thumping, but it was only Brett. All must have gone well, because he was leading the mule and it was piled high with stores. John O'Connor was lolloping alongside him, riding his new white horse. But John O'Connor wasn't bringing good news. He'd left every penny he had with Jessie Denver.

'You'd have seen it my way if you'd been there, Leo. There was the little woman in the middle of her shack, her man just buried this very morning, and this great brute of a fellow standing over her, threatening all sorts if she didn't pay for the grave and the coffin.'

'I hope your friends agree.'

They didn't. Hour after precious hour slipped away while Leo tried to persuade them. But one thing men learnt in the goldfields was that gold wasn't real until you had it in your hand. Promises meant nothing. At last one man summed it up.

'This ain't no small job! You're asking us to risk our lives, and for what? It's not our fight. This gold of yours might be real and it might be bullshit.'

'Trust me.'

'Not a chance. Not until we see real money or real gold.'

Leo despaired of them. He got to his feet.

'Do what you like. but I'm going to get Charlie.'

John O'Connor intervened.

'Listen, guys. It's way too late for you to go back to your claims today. Why not unload the mule and have a meal on us? Me and Leo will slip away to the gold-store and see if we can get you a nugget or two on account.'

He had to explain the deal several times over, but once the men had got the idea, they were agreeable. They settled down with a pack of cards to while away the afternoon, and Leo and John O'Connor rode off, leading the mule behind them.

Leo acted confidently in front of the men, but as soon as they were out of earshot, he rounded angrily on the bounty hunter.

'Are you out of your mind?'

'I've bought us time.'

'Time will change nothing. I told you, I don't know where to look for the gold.'

John O'Connor's green eyes were calm as ever.

'You've got the map. Lead the way.'

'The map's no good. It's written all in Chinese.'

'What other hope do we have?'

Leo rubbed his red and smarting eyes.

'None.'

'So we go to your Chinaman's claim, and then we pray for a miracle.'

CHAPTER TEN

Charlie's claim wasn't hard to find. It was only a couple of hours' ride from where Jake Brody had made camp, and Leo wondered how much of a coincidence that was. The claim was watered by a river, and there was a sprinkling of hardy plants and even a couple of trees. John O'Connor looked about him in the golden afternoon light.

'Nice place.'

'There's shade under those pines.'

Seeing to the horses and the mule took more precious time. John lit a fire with the fallen branches that lay around and pine-scented smoke rose in the air. Leo objected when John started cooking, but the bounty hunter shrugged off his protests.

'You need to eat. We might be working all night. Sit down and look at the map.'

Leo got out the map, but the very sight of it threw him into despair.

'I can't understand it!'

John handed him a plate of beans and a hot biscuit.

'I'm not a reading man myself. Never took to my lessons.'

Still holding the map, Leo ate hungrily. As soon as his body had fuel in it an idea came to him.

'Charlie gave me a lesson, but I don't know if I can remember it. He taught me to recognize a couple of Chinese characters.'

'Try. We need all the clues we can get.'

Leo scowled over the map while John O'Connor hung over his shoulder and breathed down his neck. The evening light turned gold and then pink while Leo struggled to make sense of the mass of markings. At first it seemed hopeless. He knew only four Chinese characters out of thousands. But he knew that he was looking for gold, and he knew the character for gold. That was enough to get him started. Leo studied the map hard, then he looked up at the lie of the land, and then he looked down at the map

124

again. The answer seemed to form in his mind like a miracle.

'The gold is near a single pine next to the river.'

'Good man!'

John's eyes blazed with excitement. He sprang to his feet and grabbed a pick from the pile of stores. He thrust a spade at Leo.

'If I'm right,' qualified Leo.

'Don't doubt yourself! Come on!'

The sun would be setting soon. The two men rushed over to a single pine-tree which stood dark against the horizon and started to hunt. The river bubbled past with a refreshing sound. Darkness fell but they kept searching for the gold. It was hard work with only lanterns to illuminate the dusty ground and piles of rock, but they couldn't wait for the light of morning. Leo's need to find the gold was desperate, but eventually he lost heart.

'I read the map wrong.'

He was answered by a jubilant shout.

'No you never! Come and look at this heathen writing!'

Leo raced over to join the bounty hunter. He was standing at a spot where the water ran deep through a cleft. John had gone into the gorge and his boots were splashing in the edge of the water. The bounty hunter lifted the lantern high to illuminate the tumble of boulders that formed the sides and bed of the river.

'Come down here. See! Scratched on the rock.'

By the light of the lantern Leo could see two Chinese characters.

The first symbol he knew, and it meant gold. The other symbol he didn't recognize. John held the lantern high and Leo looked hard at the second, baffling, meaningless character. Frustration pounded at Leo's temples.

'I can't understand the writing. And there's no time!'

John put a hand on Leo's arm.

'Steady yourself, man! Look carefully at that foreign chicken-scratch and the answer will come to you same as it did before.'

Leo wasn't so sure, but either he solved this puzzle or Jake Brody triumphed. Leo cast his mind back to his kitchen table at the Lucky LD and Charlie drawing pictures on his slate. The symbol for gold was complicated, you either knew it or you didn't. But the ones for tree and river and mountain were simpler. They looked like what they represented. Leo turned his head to look again at the single Chinese character that stood between him and success. John lifted the lamp for him. He stayed silent while Leo examined the squiggle, trying to decide whether it reminded him of anything.

'Looks like a pump handle,' he muttered at last. 'There's a little arm on the side that you could lift up and down, up and down.'

Leo looked up, and there was nothing but sky and stars above him. And the handle was pointing down. Leo looked down at the rushing river and the deep pool of water next to the boulders.

'John, can you swim?'

127

'No more than a cat can! Is that where the gold is?'

'Might be.'

Leo pulled his boots off his sore feet. His ankles were black and swollen from the fight in the stable yard.

John put down the lantern.

'I'll fetch a rope.'

Even with a rope tied around him Leo could feel the tug and pull of the water as it tried to drag him downstream. He wasn't much of a swimmer himself. He felt his way out into the deeper water. His bruised feet hit a sharp rock. The water was cold, but at least it woke him up. The icy zing of it made him forget that he'd had only a few hours' sleep the night before and looked like getting none tonight. It was getting to him, operating without sleep. If he'd had his wits about him he would have planned his search while he was sitting on a nice dry riverbank. Instead, here he was in the middle of a dark and rushing river with no idea where to start. The lanternlight swung in dizzy arcs as John called to him.

'What can you see?'

'Nothing unless you keep the light still! I'm going to start searching at the end of that big boulder.'

John settled down to keeping the light where Leo wanted it, not that Leo could see much of anything when he plunged his head into the freezing night water. Because of his broken collar-bone, his right arm wasn't much use. He clumsily used his left hand to search the smooth contours of the river-rocks that had been washed up to lie in heaps on the riverbed. It was a long cold hour. Leo's confidence in his reading of the Chinese character, never great, had deserted him entirely and he was about to give up when his searching hand brushed against a chunk of wood.

Leo forced his bursting lungs to hold on a few seconds longer, feeling his way along the shape of the wood until he was sure it was a box. He'd just touched the metal of a lock when he had to breathe or die. He rushed for the surface and sucked in air. It was a few minutes before his lungs stopped heaving and he could tell the impatient John what he'd found.

'B-box! T-there's a h-huge b-box.'

'Leo, come out and get warm before you lift it.'

'And let J-Jake B-B-Brody g-get away?'

Leo plunged back under the water. Despite the cold and the confusion of water rushing

129

around him, he found the box again straight away. He knew where it was now. He explored with his left hand. There were several boxes. The top box wasn't so very big, about three feet long by eighteen inches wide and maybe a foot deep. Leo had lifted far bigger boxes, but not under water, and not filled with the dead-weight of gold, and not with only one good hand. His first effort at lifting the box got him nowhere. And he had to breathe again, right now!

As soon as he was able, he plunged back under the water. He tried to lift the box from the bottom with his left arm, but the box was too heavy to balance and without his right arm he couldn't get any purchase. The water pulled him around as if it was his enemy and the cold sucked at his strength while he struggled. Leo couldn't bear to admit defeat, but his lungs were screaming for air, and he had to get his head above the water.

His chest heaved. His lungs wheezed as they pulled in oxygen. His forehead was split by a sharp pain. Leo clutched at the rope and tried to get in enough breath to calm his thumping heart. His bare feet slipped on the rocks as the running water tried to pull him downstream. It was even longer this time before he recovered enough to gasp out a word.

'H-h-h-h-heavy.'

'Wait!' cried the bounty hunter sharply.

Within seconds he was back, carrying a steel crowbar from their stores.

'Prise off the lid with this and fetch up a few handfuls of gold.'

Leo blessed the bounty hunter as he dived back into the freezing, tumbling water. He'd been too tired and obsessed to realize that all he needed for now was enough gold to pay the men. The heavy boxes could wait. They could come back. Leo hefted the bar in his left hand, ready to lever off the lid. Just before striking, he wondered whether the box could be full of gold-dust. What if he opened the lid and the river swept away Charlie's fortune?

He hesitated. The cold water tumbled and buffeted him, making it hard to think. He would need to breathe again soon. He had to act now. He felt for the lip of the lid of the box with his fingers. The chisel edge of the bar slipped in sweetly, the lid came off with one levering action, and, praise be! The evil force that had been sending Leo bad luck for so long had lost out this time. His cold fingers fumbled over lumpy bags of gold nuggets. He had to breathe. He rose to the surface, knowing that he was close to exhaustion, but equally that he was close to success.

John O'Connor took the crowbar and watched Leo anxiously from the bank as he coughed and shivered and sucked in air. As soon as he'd stopped panting, Leo inhaled several deep breaths to prepare himself. Although he knew it was the last time, it was hard to go into that hostile water again. He found the box of gold at once. Now that the lid was open it was the work of seconds to take out a bag full of nuggets. Leo's cold fingers would barely close around his prize, so he hugged the bag to his chest using his left arm to hold it close to him as he straightened and his gasping, shivering head came out of the water and into the night air. He was glad to see the moon rising over the horizon, showering Charlie's claim with its cool light.

John O'Connor put out the lantern and came splashing into the river to get Leo, pulling him in with the rope until he could get his arms under his left shoulder. 'Lean on me! That's the way.'

He led Leo over to the camp-fire. Leo's body

was frozen. It didn't want to fold in the middle and sit down. His hands were twice their usual size, fat and unresponsive. John O'Connor took a spare shirt from out of his saddle-bag and rubbed Leo's hands with the rough material. Leo protested when John attacked his bruised feet.

'Good! If you can feel them they ain't frozen off.'

John nipped back to the camp-fire and was back in a moment with a tin mug.

'It's only water, I can't find the tea in the dark. But it's steaming hot and it'll do you a power of good.'

Leo's teeth clattered on the rim of the mug, but his body was slowly warming. As soon as he'd drunk down the steaming-hot water Leo got to his feet and went over to the pile of his clothes which lay on the bank. His hands were clumsy, and although Jessie's bandages were still in place, his right arm wasn't helping.

'John, will you buckle on my gun?'

'Should you rest before we go back?'

'Don't tempt me!'

John O'Connor heaved a sigh.

'Sleep! Who needs it?'

He was smiling as he got to his feet. Leo was

glad of John's stout spirit. He was a man you could rely on and they were in short supply. O'Connor made Leo rest and recover while the bounty hunter packed up what they needed to take back, then he hid what they didn't need on Charlie's claim. He organized the gold into what they needed to pay for the men and concealed the rest. He tacked up the horses and then he insisted on leading Leo's horse, saying that Leo could nap as he rode.

'I won't sleep!' Leo protested.

But Leo was soon aware of his head nodding and he slipped in and out of an uncomfortable doze during most of the two-hour ride down the trail back to where they'd left the men. John woke him before they rounded the side of a hill and the track opened out down towards the spot where the men should be waiting. Despite John's optimism, Leo couldn't be easy in his mind until he saw the pinprick of a camp-fire.

'I told you they'd wait,' John said cheerfully.

It was a relief to see that the hired crew were still there. Now Leo's next task rushed up to slap him in the face. He'd probably think better for some sleep, but there was no time. He'd have to do the best he could. At least the men were delighted with the nuggets. Calloused dirty hands closed over their prizes.

'Same again if we get my friend back alive,' Leo promised.

The men would have ridden out at once, but Leo told them to sleep for a few hours, while he scouted out Brody's camp. O'Connor insisted on coming with him.

'Stay back then, John. If they have a guard out, I might need your backup!'

O'Connor nodded agreement and Leo went ahead. The ground was so open that there was nothing he could do to hide his approach, but he moved carefully, ready to drop to the ground if he saw or heard anything. The track led uphill. The smell of smoke warned him he was getting close to Brody's camp. Leo could hear the river over to his right. A few spindly bushes spread out towards Leo. He made the most of their cover as he moved silently over the last few yards.

Once over the top of the ridge the ground fell away into nothing. Wary of his silhouette in the moonlight, Leo lay flat along the top of the ridge and peered over cautiously. Below him was a bowl-shaped depression in the ground, ringed the whole way around by high ground. In the

centre of the depression were three scruffy tents,
a line of washing and a row of tethered horses.
Dark forms slept around a camp-fire that was
nearly out.

Leo's first feeling was that Jake Brody was
mad! It went against every military instinct to
have a camp in the middle of such low ground.
A few men with rifles on the high ground could
hold the low-lying camp hostage in an instant.
But a second thought showed him Brody's
plans. Jake thought he was in no danger of an
attack from a horde of men. He had been trying
to prevent one lone person from getting close,
and for that, this site was perfect. If Leo had
tried a solo rescue he wouldn't have been able
to approach anywhere along the bare sides of
the depression without standing out like a
mouse in a sugar bowl. But Leo wasn't going to
attack alone. He had John O'Connor and a
bunch of hired men. Brody had underestimated
him, and Leo was going to make him pay for
that mistake.

Leo slipped back and briefed O'Connor, then
they went back to wake up the men. With gold
in their hands, and recovered from their hang-
overs, the men were thirsting for action. Leo
crouched down and drew a map of Brody's

camp in the dust.

'We'll space ourselves around the top of the ridge, wait for them to wake up, and then I'll do the talking.'

'You want us to hide?'

'No. I want him to know that he's trapped. But don't make yourselves targets!'

Already another dawn was lightening the sky in the east. Leo made the men hurry into position, but then they had an hour with nothing to do but watch the moon set and the sun rise before the first man – the ratlike Stan – got up from the ground by the ashes of the camp-fire and walked a few yards away for a leak.

Leo saw the hats of his men bob excitedly, but he gestured them to wait. It was Brody he wanted to talk to. A few seconds later Brody's bull-like figure heaved itself up from the ground by the fire. He didn't bother to move away. He relieved himself right in the middle of the ashes. Leo didn't wait for him to finish.

'Jake Brody! I got you surrounded. All of you, put your hands in the air!'

Stan's hands shot up, but Jake Brody's massive head whipped around as he stared in every direction. His hand automatically went to his gun-belt. But Leo knew that he would be able to count nine men and nine rifles, and he wasn't surprised when Jake's hand fell away again. Brody didn't raise his hands in surrender. Leo wasn't worried. The hard part had been setting up the ambush. He knew in his heart that Brody was beaten. Leo's tone was almost lazy as he issued his orders.

'Throw down your guns and put your hands in the air!'

A well-muscled figure rushed out of one of the tents, and the stupid man was carrying a rifle. God alone knew what he thought he was doing. Gunshots cracked and he fell to the ground, hit by half a dozen shots at the same time. Now two more of Brody's hired guns showed themselves, but they had no intention of fighting. They both held out their gunbelts to show they were surrendering, threw them to the ground well out of reach, then raised their hands. Leo waited. The moment was sweet. At last Jake Brody threw down his gun. Slowly, his hands went up in the air.

'Yah hey! We got them!'

There was nothing Leo could do to stop his hired men running down the sides of the ridge and down into the camp ground. They were excited. One of them put an extra shot into the muscle-man's head, although there was no possible chance that he was alive. Leo and John O'Connor followed more carefully, unwilling to let carelessness ruin their success. But their party was in complete control. Leo let the men line up Brody, Stan and the two strangers, but he didn't let them kill them. Not yet. Despite the eight guns already trained on the captives, Leo lifted his own gun – it felt odd in his left hand – and pointed it at Brody. He wanted to know what had befallen the Chinaman before he meted out punishment.

'John, will you look for Charlie?'

While he waited for the bounty hunter to come back, Leo looked directly into Jake Brody's eyes. The man was seething in a mean and baffled fury. He was so used to being powerful that he didn't realize that he was beaten. The cold blue eyes were so threatening that Leo reminded himself to stay on his guard. Even now, Brody was a dangerous man.

'Hey, Leo! Brody told me you were dead!'

Charlie stood grinning, happiness glowing in his black eyes, rubbing his hands together to get the circulation going. Leo could see red rope-marks on the slight wrists, but he was glad to see that Charlie looked fine. Except for one detail.

'Charlie! Your pigtail!'

The Chinaman's face went stern and he pointed at the ratlike Stan.

'He cut my hair. I've got business with that man.'

'What about the others?'

'Nothing extra.'

Leo looked at the two strangers. They were sweating with fear and he could smell last night's whiskey on them. It was plain that they thought Leo would shoot them.

'We met Jake Brody in town, is all,' one volunteered. 'We ain't no part of your quarrel with him.'

Leo made his mind up.

'If I let you go, you'll keep moving?'

'On my mother's life.'

'Oh, mister! I promise!'

'Pick your employer more carefully next time! You got thirty seconds. Leave your guns. Go direct to your horses, and get moving.'

The two men ran for their horses. They stopped for nothing, but untied the horses, jumped on Indian-style and galloped off. They were obviously not used to riding without saddles. They flopped around like freshly caught fish.

'They ride worse than you, Charlie.'

Charlie was watching Stan, who had made a movement towards the line of horses.

'You're going nowhere!' the Chinaman ordered.

Jake Brody gestured that he wanted to ride away.

Leo snapped: 'You stay put!'

He saw astonishment in the cold blue eyes. Even now Jake didn't realize that he could no longer squash Leo like an irritating bug. His tone was arrogant.

'You can't give me orders, Denver!'

Now that the moment of revenge was here Leo found that he took no pleasure in it.

'Jake, how exactly do you aim to stop me?'

Leo looked long and hard at Brody, letting the man know that he'd been judged and found guilty. Brody's eyes met Leo's, and at last, Leo saw the bully crumble.

'What have you got against me?' he whined.

'You have to ask?'

'You can't shoot me. We're from the same town.'

Leo lifted his gun. For all that he knew Jake Brody richly deserved death, shooting an unarmed grovelling man felt uncomfortably like

141

an execution. It was as much to stiffen his own resolve as to enlighten Jake that Leo recited his crimes.

'You killed my brother! You kidnapped my friend!'

'No! Don't kill me!' howled Brody.

Jake flung himself to his knees and made as if he would clutch in the direction of Leo's boots. But then he got up from his knees and turned the assault into a charge. His attack freed Leo from his inhibitions and he fired the first bullet easily, the second bullet calmly and the third bullet with purpose. Jake Brody lay dead at his feet.

'Nasty piece of work,' said one of Leo's crew.

The others were looking at Charlie. The Chinaman stood triumphant over the fallen figure of Stan. The ratlike head lay at an unnatural angle to the neck. John O'Connor was astounded.

'How did you do that with your bare hands? I only turned away for a second. Did you see that, Leo?'

'I missed it.'

Charlie grinned.

'The Flash of Lightning, that's me.'

John O'Connor regarded the Chinaman for a

long astonished moment and then he threw
back his head and howled with laughter.

And Leo found himself laughing as well.

CHAPTER ELEVEN

Jessie asked no awkward questions when Leo, Charlie and John returned to her shack. She accepted the Chinaman as easily as she accepted the heavy boxes they hid under her bed. Knowing how dangerous it would be if word of the gold got out, Leo was on fire to start back to Hope Town. Jessie didn't want to leave the gold-fields.

'I have the Lord's work to do. How can I abandon the miners to sin and poverty?'

Leo knew from his dealings with Theodore that there was no arguing with a missionary's sense of duty. Maybe if he appealed to it?

'I hate to think of my nephew growing up better than a thousand miles from me.'

Jessie's brow furrowed.

'Is there a church in Hope Town?'

Leo's heart sank, but he wouldn't tell his sister-in-law a lie.

'I'm sorry. There ain't.'

To his surprise, Jessie's beautiful eyes cleared and she smiled at him.

'Then my duty is plain. I can bring the word of the Lord to the sinners in Hope and you can be near your nephew.'

They still couldn't get going. New boxes had to be made for the gold because the old ones were rotten. Then they had to see Charlie safely onto a stagecoach that was heading East. Leo made sure that the two men Charlie hired from the rescue crew to act as guards knew that retribution would be swift and terrible if they let harm come to the Chinaman. Then there was further delay while Jessie decided which poor family was most deserving of the shack, but at last they were free to take stagecoach out of town.

Leo and John O'Connor kept their rifles to hand and a sharp eye out. The journey was long, bumpy and boring. Leo thought of Charlie's intention to build a railway.

'The Chinaman will make millions!' he told O'Connor, his teeth rattling as he spoke. 'This is worse than going to the dentist!'

The bounty hunter grimaced.

'Goes on longer too. How many days further?'

'Another three. Give me the baby, Mrs Denver. It's your turn to sleep.'

Truth be told, Leo didn't reckon much to his nephew. Stagecoach travel didn't agree with the little mite any more than it did with Leo, but the baby had no inhibitions about making its displeasure known!

As soon as they got to Hope Town Leo sent Jessie back to the Lucky LD with John O'Connor to watch over her and the baby. Then he hired Buck Harper and Sam Turner from the stables to help him carry the gold to the bank. Clarence Carnegie was so excited by the idea of boxes full of gold nuggets that he quivered and clucked like an old hen. Sam and Buck showed no signs of going back to work, but hung around hoping to see the fun. The bank door banged in a hurry and Willy Sticks hobbled in.

'Hey, Leo! You gonna count that gold of yours?'

Leo couldn't help smiling. It was good to be home. But he made Jim Brady shoo out the watchers and then lock the door before he would open the boxes. Clarence was so overcome that Jim had to do all the weighing and counting, His eyes were shining with excitement as he came to the total.

'Makes you the richest man in Hope, Mr Denver.'

'Saving Jake Brody's estate.'

'No, sir, that's where you're wrong. Brody got to speculating and lost everything his daddy left him and more. His place is on the market now.'

'How much?'

Jim named a sum that wouldn't even dent the amount that had just been credited to Leo's account. Leo could buy out Brody any time he wanted.

'Do we have a new lawyer in town yet?'

'Yes, sir. Wilson Watkins hung out a shingle a week or so back. He's OK. His sister is married to Sam Turner.'

'Tell the lawyer I'll be round to see him tomorrow.'

'I thought you would, sir. It's a good ranch.'

'Keep it to yourself, Jim. You, too, Carnegie!'

'Yes, sir.'

'Yes, sir. Oh, Mr Denver, sir. It's so exciting to have you back! We knew you'd want to buy Brody's land.'

'Not a word until I've spoken with his widow.'

Leo was dreading his interview with Rose Brody so he put it off until the next day and went home. The Lucky LD was in apple-pie order. Leo was unstinting in his praise to Nathan, who flushed crimson with delight. Hank Miller had done a fine job of weeding out the scrub bulls and his Mexican lady had the house in sparkling order.

'There's a place with me as long as you want it,' Leo reassured them.

Hank's face split in a relieved smile.

'That's mighty grand of you, Mr Denver.'

Leo wasn't sure if he liked being 'Mr Denver, sir' to so many people or not. It didn't seem that long since he was a trail hand. However his new status had advantages. He was already feeling the need for a new house, for example. His simple cabin was crowded to the rafters, even with John O'Connor insisting that he wanted to sleep in the barn. Leo was surprised.

'You'll be wanting to join me after one night,' John prophesied.

And sure enough, after half a night crammed into the tiny cabin with his nephew waking every hour on the hour and Hank snoring like a buffalo, Leo fetched out his bed-roll and joined John in the barn.

In the morning Leo went to the horse corral. His palomino mare lifted her head as soon as she saw him. She snorted and whinnied out loud, then she came trotting over. 'We got business in town, girl. Fancy a trip out?'

Sunshine nuzzled at his hand and didn't mind showing that she was delighted to have him home. Riding his own sweet mare was some consolation to Leo on the awful ride to the Brodys' spread. It wasn't Leo's fault Brody had lost his money by speculating, and if Brody had stayed home and tried to recover his fortune in an honest way then Leo wouldn't have had to shoot him, but none of this made Leo feel better about facing his widow.

Rose was trying on a feathered black hat in front of the mirror when he was ushered into the Brodys' ornate parlour. She threw the hat on the table and ran to Leo. She looked so happy that Leo thought she couldn't know her husband was dead and that he'd have to tell her. But her first words made it plain that she knew.

'Is it true that Jake is dead and you shot him?'

Leo gripped his own hat between his hands.

'Ma'am, Mrs Brody. I'm sorry to say that is about the truth of it.'

Rose's blue eyes sparkled and she clapped her

hands in glee.

'Famous! Now we can be married!'

'Uh, married? You and me?'

'Yes, married, stupid! You asked me often enough, Leo Denver! Now that you're rich you can have me! We'll have to wait for the wedding, or those cats in town will gossip. But you can move in to the house right away, Leo! Together at last!'

Leo gazed at Rose's pretty face. He felt himself in the worst spot of his life.

'I can't rightly do that while you're in mourning, Rose.'

'Don't be silly, Leo! I'm real happy Jake's gone! He was that mean to me you wouldn't believe it! Why, he told me to wash my own clothes! You wouldn't be such a tightwad, would you, Leo?'

She took a step towards him, smiling. Leo backed away from her advance. The code of a gentleman warred with his desire to escape!

'Things change, Rose. Are you still sure me and you would suit?'

The blue eyes narrowed and Leo saw a mean expression that chilled his heart.

'You got another think coming, Denver, if you imagine you're gonna weasel out of marrying me! You killed two men to get me! You can't change your mind now!'

He was trapped! Or was he?

'Very well, Rose. I'll move in with my sister-in-law, my nephew, my friend John O'Connor and Hank Miller and his Mexican wife in the morning.'

Rose's jaw dropped in horror. Leo had a further stroke of inspiration.

'I'm hoping Charlie Tang will be visiting soon. I told him and his family that my house was theirs so long as I lived.'

And not a word of it was untrue. Leo watched Rose recoil from him in consternation. Her blue eyes were shocked.

'You can't be serious?'

'Never more so, Rose. We'd best get the rules clear from the start. You will be washing your own clothes, and where I go my friends and family go. And don't think you can fight me. A man ought to be boss in his own home.'

Leo watched the blue eyes narrow as Rose calculated her best move.

'You'd be horrid to live with,' she pronounced at last.

Leo didn't disagree.

'Well, then, I won't marry you! I'll have

Clarence Carnegie instead! He's the next richest man in the area, and I'd kind of like to live in the town! It gets awful dull out here with nothing but cows for company!'

'I think you'll be very happy, Rose.'

'Why didn't I think of moving to town before? I hate this ranch. Are you going to buy it?'

'I'll be building a new house. This one is yours as long as you wish.'

'That's good. Mamma can stay with the brats. I don't want them living with me.'

Rose moved over to the mirror and resumed her experiments with the hat. Leo scarcely dared believe he'd escaped so lightly. Rose managed to get her hat on at exactly the right angle and she made a satisfied sound before turning around.

'What do you think?'

'I don't know a lot about hats. Is your mother home? I'd like to pay my respects.'

'How dull! Well, if you must.'

Mrs Denver was in the parlour and her eyes were red from weeping. Leo hesitated uncomfortably in the doorway. She waddled over to him and held his hands in a pudgy, sweaty grip.

'Oh, Leo! Jake was so good to us, even if he did lose all his money, which could happen to

152

anyone. Killing and kidnapping is very wrong and I suppose he had to be punished. But how many men would make a good home for a poor widow woman like me? Jake took all my children in, and I'm sure he never meant to lose his temper with them. I nearly died when I heard you were buying his land, but then of course I realized that you'd be marrying Rose so everything's all right.'

'Mrs Prescott, ma'am, Rose and me have agreed that we shouldn't suit.'

Her shriek made his ears ring.

'Lord! Have you come to turn us all out?'

She burst into such noisy sobs that she couldn't hear Leo's assurances. The door burst open and Jasmine flew in.

'Mamma? What's w-wrong?'

Jasmine administered sal volatile to her mother, got her to lie on the sofa and fanned her vigorously and even then it was some time before Mrs Prescott subsided into slightly quieter, gasping, hiccuping sobs. Leo seized his chance.

'I promise you, ma'am. I ain't turning nobody out. This house is yours.'

Jasmine looked at Leo and he saw that although the slanting brows were the same, the expression in her dark eyes was subdued and she too had been crying.

'What do you m-mean, Leo? You'll be l-living here with Rose, won't you?'

Rose stuck her head into the room. She looked beautiful. The black feathers of the hat curled enchantingly around her blond hair. Her blue eyes were untroubled.

'Don't be more of a fool that you can help, Jasmine! I'm marrying Clarence Carnegie! I'm taking the buggy and going into town to tell him of his good fortune!'

Rose vanished. Mrs Prescott burst into loud and noisy sobs again, but this time Leo gathered it was because she was so happy about the wedding.

'I'll see you to the door, Leo,' said Jasmine. 'I'll have to stay with M-Mamma this afternoon. But may I come and see the b-baby?'

'Be glad to have you over,' Leo said.

He put on his hat and walked to the hitching-post where Sunshine waited. Jasmine suddenly rushed after him in her old harum-scarum way. Her hair had grown into pretty curls. She looked happier than she had a few minutes ago. Her eyes sparkled.

Leo smiled down at her. An attractive pink

flush stained her cheeks, and he saw her take a breath before she spoke, but her words still rocked him out of his boots.

'Leo, if you aren't having Rose, will you m-marry me instead?'

Leo turned to his palomino to cover his confusion. He unhitched his mare and patted her nose. Horses were a darn sight easier to cope with than women!

'Leo?'

'The man's supposed to do the asking! And as it happens, I was aiming to ask a certain person to marry me.'

Jasmine's curly head drooped.

'I'm s-sorry, Leo. I never get being a l-lady right. I didn't know that you l-loved someone else.'

'The woman I love is a perfect lady,' Leo said softly.

'I h-hope you'll be very h-happy.'

Leo laughed.

'I'll be the happiest man in the world. I know that because if I was miserable or in trouble of any kind, my lady would turn the world upside down to save me.'

Jasmine said no more but turned towards the house, and Leo suddenly gave up on teasing her. He caught her and drew her back towards him.

'Jasmine Prescott, will you marry me?'

She could hardly believe him.

'M-me?'

He smiled into her dark eyes, watching the clouds clear and happiness dawn as she read the love in his expression.

'I think I've loved you ever since you stole that donkey.'

Her smile lifted her mouth and her eyes sparkled.

'Don't remind me!'

'Or maybe it was when you cut off all your hair.'

'Leo!'

He drew her to him. She made a sweet armful. He kissed the tip of her nose.

'I'm glad you look nothing like a boy.'

Jasmine stood on her tiptoes and kissed his lips in a way that made it clear she was a woman and not a little girl any more. Leo returned the kiss, then held her at arm's length. Her eyes were laughing.

'Told you I was grown up!'

'Urrgh! Sloppy stuff!' piped up a voice beside them. 'Hi Leo. Will you tell that Matt Brody that I killed a Mexican? He won't believe me. I told him that you've got loads of gold and that he's gonna have to live in the orphanage now Jake's dead because you're buying this house, but he won't believe that either.'

Leo reluctantly let go of Jasmine. Matt Brody stood next to Jason. He was overweight and looked spoilt and miserable, yet deep in the lad's eyes Leo saw a spark of character that gave him hope. He spoke as warmly as he could.

'Glad to meet you, Matt. You don't have to go to the orphanage. You can make your home with us. But you'll have to get along better with Jason. He don't tell no lies, and I sure hope you won't either.'

Matt gave him a thankful look. He and Jason ran off together. Jasmine slipped her arm through Leo's and gazed at him with loving eyes.

'Did you see the way Matt looked at you? I never saw such h-hero worship.'

'Maybe we can straighten him out.'

'You'll be a better role model for him than Jake Brody was. Oh, Leo. I can't believe how h-happy I am.'

Leo would have kissed her again, but Mrs Prescott yoo-hooed from the doorway of the house. Jasmine looked at her mother and then at Leo.

'Mamma will cry when I tell her we're getting m-married.'

'I got urgent business in town.'

Jasmine's eyes were understanding. She grinned and waved him away.

' 'Bye, Leo. Tell Mrs Denver I'll bring her some b-baby clothes when I come.'

Leo felt great as he rode Sunshine into town to see Lawyer Watkins. It seemed that fortune was smiling kindly on him at last. His business with the lawyer went smoothly. Leo would be taking possession of his new ranch in such a short time that he thought he'd better call in at the lumber yard and reserve some timber and a crew.

'I ain't got no plans yet,' he told the carpenter, old Joshua Troop. 'I'd like to talk the style over with Jas- that is, with my sister-in-law, before I commence building.'

'No problem, Mr Denver, sir. Where will you site the new house?'

'You know that stand of white pine by the gulch?'

'Above the river? Best place for a house. I always thought Brody was crazy building where he did.'

Leo was whistling as he unhitched his palomino and rode back to the Lucky LD. The one thing that spoilt his pleasure was catching

sight of a poster urging the townsfolk to vote for
Sheriff Wicks in the forthcoming elections. Leo
felt that his account with Wicks was not settled,
but although he pondered the matter all the way
home he couldn't think how to repay the man.
The answer didn't come to him until later that
evening, when John O'Connor started to talk of
leaving.

'Make your home with us, John.'

'I've reached a time in me life when I would-
n't mind settling down. But a man must be doing
something, and ranching isn't me, Leo.'

John's eyes rested on Jessie as he spoke. She
made a sweet domestic picture nursing her baby
by the fire. Leo spoke sincerely to his friend.

'I'd like it fine if you could stay, John.'

'And so would I. But I don't know how to do
anything but catch the bad fellas.'

Leo's bright idea exploded in his mind like a
firework.

'John O'Connor. How would you like to be
sheriff of Hope Town?'